PHARAOH'S TOMB

Crystal Journals: Book 2

G. Rosemary Ludlow

This is a work of fiction. All of the characters, organizations, and events portrayed in this novel are either the products of the author's imagination or are used fictitiously.

Summary: As the Guardian of the Crystal of the North, young Susan Sinclair must help restore balance throughout history. But can she survive the incredible adventure awaiting her in ancient Egypt?

Library and Archives Canada Cataloguing in Publication

G. Rosemary Ludlow
Crystal Journals Bk 2: Pharaoh's Tomb

ISBN: 0973687134
ISBN 13: 9780973687132

I. Title

1. Ancient Egypt 2. Middle Grade History 3. Time Travel
4. Action and Adventure 5. Educational Stories

Published by: Comwave Publishing House Inc,
Vancouver, BC, Canada

For Steve

My Dad, who gave me a lasting love and respect for learning.

ACKNOWLEDGMENTS

So many people contribute to the creation of a book.

With this one I wish to acknowledge all those people who gave me encouragement along the way. It's sometimes hard to know you can do it when you haven't done it yet.

People bought and read my first book A Rare Gift. A heartfelt thank-you to you all. Many reviewed it and a big thank you for that.

There is no greater encouragement and validation than for people to read what you wrote and let you know that they enjoyed it and want more.

THE STORY SO FAR

A Rare Gift, tells the story of how Susan Sinclair receives a crystal from a lady at a flea market. The lady gives it to her, but it is even more correct to say that the crystal chose Susan. Unfortunately Susan doesn't wait to hear what is important about the crystal but wanders off into the crowd.

She wakes up on a sailing ship tossed in the Atlantic. Susan has no idea where she is or how she got there, but she does know that she doesn't like it. And she doesn't like the boy who sneers at her and accuses her of trying to steal his knife.

In a later meeting with the lady, Mrs. Coleman, Susan learns that she is now the Guardian of the Crystal of the North and that it will lead her to places where there is an imbalance or unfairness in the world and that she will be able to help correct the situation.

When she learns that she is expected to help the nasty knife-wielding boy, Susan is not at all interested in being a Guardian, but that is now her destiny. The ship is carrying immigrants from England to New York. The boy, Jeremy, started the voyage with his family, but one by one they died of fever, and so Jeremy is left alone and friendless and very much in need of help.

Susan gradually grows into her role and Jeremy and Susan have many adventures and help a lot of children before the first story is fully told.

And now you are ready for Susan's second adventure with her crystal.

CAST OF CHARACTERS

There are many more people in this book than in book 1. Also, in Ancient Egypt one person could have as many as three names. Especially kings and nobles.

I have created a "Cast of Characters." You can refer to it if you need to.

In Present Time

Judy Green, Susan's friend

Miranda Coleman, prior Guardian of the Crystal of the North

The Sinclair family
Susan Sinclair, Guardian of the Crystal of the North

Alice Sinclair, Susan's mother
Stewart Sinclair, Susan's father
Aunt Laura, Jason's mother
Uncle John, Jason's father
Jason, Susan's cousin

In Ancient Egypt

Ahmose, shortened name for the grand vizier, Djus's father

Akheperenre, throne name of Tuthmoses II

Amehtu-Ahmose, full name of the grand vizier, Djus's father

Baqt'e, friend of Neferure—a good swimmer

Dauuf, friend of Djus

Djus, nickname for Useramen, son of the grand vizier, and Susan's friend

Hatshepsut, great wife of Tuthmoses II, daughter of Tuthmoses I, mother of Neferure, regent for Tuthmoses III

Harsheer, court magician and high priest.

Hery Seshesta, title of the chief embalmer

Hori, one of Harsheer's soldiers

Merimose, General, Pawara's general

Merit-Amen, Princess, Egyptian name of Susan Sinclair

Miew, helper sent to Merit-Amen by Djus's mother

Nebka, friend of Djus

Neferure, daughter of Hatshepsut and Tuthmoses II

Nozme, Harsheer's housekeeper on his estate

Pawara, governor, southern province, and friend of Tuthmoses II

Peri, friend of Neferure

Senmut, a palace official

Takaret, priestess of Ma'at in Thebes

Teo, Susan's maid

Tuthmoses I, throne name Aakheperkara, father of Tuthmoses II and Hatshepsut

Tuthmoses II, throne name Akheperenre, husband and half brother of Hatshepsut, father of Neferure and Tuthmoses III

Tuthmoses III, throne name—Menkheperenre, son of Tuthmoses II

Useramen, Djus, son of the grand vizier, Susan's friend

CHAPTER 1

WHY IS THE PAPER BLANK?

"That's very weird, Susan. Are you sure?"

"Yes, of course I'm sure." Susan nodded, even though she was on the phone.

"I don't understand it." Mrs. Coleman sounded puzzled on the other end of the line. "Go over what happened step by step."

Susan sighed but told her story again.

"I opened the envelope you gave me; I pulled out the paper; I unfolded it; the paper was blank."

"That's impossible." Mrs. Coleman sounded totally certain.

"I didn't do anything to the paper; I just looked at it, and there was nothing on it." Susan felt as if it were her fault the paper was blank.

"Look, Susan, don't worry about it," Mrs. Coleman reassured her. "Maybe this is the beginning of your next adventure or something."

"Did you have a crystal journey start like this?" Susan asked, curious.

"No. Never. The paper didn't change the whole time I had it – except for some blood that dripped on one corner once."

Susan peered at a corner of the paper. "The blood is still here. I can see that."

"Then it's the correct piece of paper. I wonder where the writing went. How exciting. I do envy you."

"Well, I've had one adventure already, and I still don't even know what the crystal's instructions are. It's like trying to work the DVD without looking in the manual."

"Yes," said Mrs. Coleman, "I can understand how that would worry you. Let me think. OK, it goes like this. Your crystal was made by a magician a long time ago. Nobody knows his name or where he came from. The paper you're holding is papyrus, which was made in Egypt in ancient times, but that's the only clue. Anyway, he made four crystals. They're to be used to correct the balance when things go wrong. The person who is the Guardian of the Crystal—you're one of them now—is drawn to the area of unbalance and corrects it. This usually means helping someone. You are the Guardian of the Crystal of the North."

Susan sighed. The title sounded so grand.

"Thank you, but that's a lot to expect. Four people to correct everything in the world that goes wrong."

"Not everything, Susan. The crystal never expects you to do more than you can. After all, watch any newscast and you can see that not everything is being corrected. But as a Guardian, you will do what you can."

"How do you know that?"

"That's easy." Mrs. Coleman laughed. "You wouldn't be a Guardian if you couldn't or wouldn't do what you can. The crystal picked you, remember?"

Susan did remember. She remembered being very angry and trying to give the crystal back to Mrs. Coleman at the flea market. And she remembered how thrilled she had been when she finally realized that the crystal was hers and that she could use it to help others.

Susan heard a slight scuffle behind her and, glancing in the hallway mirror, saw her friend Judy trying to creep up behind her. Quickly she stuffed the paper and envelope into the front of her sweater.

"Oh, I have to go now. Thanks for the advice," Susan said quickly.

"Call again if you want to talk some more about it. Good luck," said Mrs. Coleman and hung up.

"Who was that?" Judy wanted to know. "You sure were talking heavy there, Sue Sue. What's going on? Hey, look at your hair. I swear its growing daily."

They moved to the hall mirror.

I need a haircut. Susan screwed up her face.

"Sue Sue, it's really grown." Judy held out a hank of Susan's ash-brown hair. She stretched it gently to get the wave out and laid her hand along the tress to measure it.

"It's longer than my hand already. I wish my hair grew so fast."

Susan wished Judy wouldn't call her Sue Sue. She hated it. In the mirror she saw her snubby nose and her freckles and her blue, blue eyes. She saw Judy, too. Judy was so pretty.

"It'll be great. You'll be able to do so much more with it once it's longer. Put it up, braid it. You'll look great."

Susan didn't care about all that stuff, but Judy found it important, and Susan was willing to go along. She was glad when the doorbell rang and Judy rushed to answer it. It gave her a chance to slip the envelope and paper into the drawer of the phone table. *I must remember to hide it later,* she thought as she hurried after Judy to the door.

CHAPTER 2

A LETTER

Mrs. Gliddan, the letter carrier, stood on the porch.

"Hi, honey, I have a registered letter for Alice Sinclair. Is she at home?"

"She's in her studio out back," said Susan. "I can sign for it."

"Oh boy, I bet it's important." Judy took the letter and shook it up to her ear. She held it up to the light.

"I can't see anything. Quick. I wonder what it can be."

Susan quickly shut the door and hurried after Judy who was already in the mudroom and heading out the back door.

The studio was an old barn the Sinclairs had turned into a large, open area where Mrs. Sinclair could work on her sculptures. Windows occupied the whole south wall from floor to ceiling so that the studio flooded with light all day long.

Susan and Judy rushed into the studio together.

Susan's mother sat on a stool, picking away at a block of marble. The block towered above her, black, with streaks of white and silver running through it. *Tap, tap*, went her hammer, and then she stopped to examine the marks she had made. *Tap, tap* again, and she blew out the chips and looked again, cocking her head to the side to get different angles on the cut. She was so absorbed in her work that she didn't notice the clamor of the approaching girls until Judy thrust the letter almost under her nose.

"Goodness." She gasped in surprise.

"Sorry, Mrs. S," said Judy. "Quick. Open the letter. We want to know what's happening." Judy hopped with impatience. "Quick, quick."

Susan wanted to know what the letter said, too. She hoped for good news. She hung back a little, though. She leaned against her own workbench set up in one corner of the studio.

"Oh goodness." Mrs. Sinclair quickly ripped the envelope and scanned the letter inside.

Judy strained to read over her shoulder, but Susan watched her mother's face. First she saw embarrassment, then sadness and then worry. Finally her mother looked up, smiling.

"What is it?" Susan asked.

Mrs. Sinclair came over to Susan's bench and leaned next to her so Susan could see the letter.

"It's from your uncle John."

Susan nodded. She remembered Uncle John. He had moved to Australia.

"Well, he married a lady, Aunt Laura, who already had a son called Jason."

Susan nodded; she knew that.

Judy nodded; she knew that, too. She had seen photos.

"Jason has cancer, and they've come from Australia to North America for some special treatment."

Susan hadn't known that.

"Jason is resting before his next round of treatment, so they're coming to stay for a few weeks, and I forgot all about it." Mrs. Sinclair looked down at Susan with a question in her eyes.

"Ace." Judy thought it was a good idea.

Susan stirred herself. *Yes, that will be good. It must be awful to be so sick and so far away from home.*

"It will be nice to meet Jason," she said.

"Susan, it will be like having a brother, like I've got Darren. Wow, we'll have so much fun together." Judy jumped up and down with excitement.

Susan felt skeptical about that. She profoundly hoped Jason and Darren were very different. What if the crystal called her while he was visiting? It was going to be hard to hide from him. What if Jason saw her disappear and told on her? She didn't want to have a fight with him like she had had with Judy. It had taken a couple of weeks before they were friends again.

"This is awful. I forgot all about it," said Mrs. Sinclair. "I get so busy when I've got a new marble to work on. It just slipped my mind." She turned to leave, crumpling the letter in her hand.

Susan sighed. *Mum is always so absentminded.*

"When do they arrive?" she asked.

"Tomorrow morning, early," her mother answered as she hurried out.

"Hey, I haven't seen this one." Judy poked her finger at the work laid out on Susan's bench. She picked up a lump of soapstone. Susan's latest carving. "What is it?"

"It's nothing," said Susan taking it from her and rubbing it gently. "I just like to make a nice shape that feels good in my hands."

Judy took it back and tried it. She enclosed the stone in her hands. She ran her thumb along the first groove Susan had carved.

"Oh, Susan, I think you're so clever to be able to do this stuff." Judy shut her eyes. "It feels so good. Do you think you'll teach Jason how to do it, too? How sick is he, do you think? Do you think he'll like biking down to the river with us?"

Susan sighed again. *I hope I don't get pulled away on a crystal journey right in front of him.* That was her biggest worry.

"I think we'll just have to wait and see," she said.

"I'm coming over early tomorrow to meet him. Then we can suss him out. I've never met anyone from Australia; do you think we'll be able to understand what he says? It's so exciting."

Judy reached to put the soapstone carving back on the bench between the files and sandpaper that littered the top. She gave a little gasp and peered closely at a saucer on the corner of the bench. A stone rested in the middle of the saucer and tiny crystals grew on the stone.

"Hey, you tried growing crystals," Judy said. "These are pretty. I like them a lot."

"They're pretty," agreed Susan, "but they're so small. I can't get them to grow big, no matter what."

Judy looked at her. "Remember, I showed you. Darren takes the little crystal and hangs it in the solution. Remember it was in a jar on his desk."

And then Susan did remember. She nodded.

Then Judy completely surprised Susan by saying, "You had a bigger crystal, Susan. What happened to it? I haven't seen it for ages. I thought you liked it."

Susan looked sideways at Judy. Her crystal—the Crystal of the North—stood right beside the saucer with the crystals. It was in full view, and Judy should have seen it.

It's true what Mrs. Coleman says, thought Susan. *Most people really don't see the crystal. Any closer and it would have poked Judy in the nose.*

Susan quietly picked it up and slipped it into her pocket. At the same time, hoping to distract Judy, Susan pointed to her mother's new marble block. "Do you like the new statue?"

"What's it going to be?" Judy wanted to know. She cocked her head to the side as she looked at the grooves in the marble.

"Here's the sketches." Susan drew Judy farther away from her workbench.

"It's going to be a killer whale," Judy said with delight. "It looks great. I love it when they leap out of the water like that." The sketch showed a killer whale, flopping into the sea on its back, with its white belly exposed. All around the tail and along the lower part of its back was a huge splash of water, and the orca seemed to have a smile on its face.

"It's going in the square in front of the library when it's finished," Susan told Judy as she moved her toward the door.

The two of them left the studio, closing the door behind them.

CHAPTER 3

THIS IS DIFFERENT

That evening, over supper, all the conversation was about the visitors.

"I wish I'd had a little more warning." Mr. Sinclair shook his head ruefully. "Really, Alice, you should write things down."

"I meant to write it down, Stewart, but I forgot." Susan's mother shrugged and smiled. Her forgetfulness was an old joke in the family.

"We'll need to leave for the airport very early tomorrow morning. Susan, I think it's best if you sleep in. With three extra people and all their luggage, it's going to be tight in the van." Susan's father smiled, too.

Susan nodded. She listened as her father planned out the run to the airport; and where everyone was going to sleep; and how they needed to get extra blankets from the attic. She was pushing broccoli around her plate, trying to make it disappear when she felt a wave of dizziness.

Is this what fainting feels like? she wondered. She dropped her fork. It made a loud clatter on the edge of her plate.

"Suzie, you look as white as a sheet." Her father reached over and felt her forehead. "Hmm, no fever."

Susan felt stretched away. She gripped the edge of the table. *I will not disappear in front of my parents,* she thought fiercely.

"It must be all the excitement," Susan's mother added.

"Yes, that's it," Susan said, getting up from the table. "I'm all right, really. But I think I'll go to bed early—like now." She hurried across the kitchen. The movement seemed to help her to steady. She turned in the doorway.

"I'll see you when you get back from the airport. Good night."

Her parents exchanged looks as she left the room.

Susan heard her mother say, "I hope she isn't upset about Jason coming."

"Not our Suzie Loose Goose. She'll be fine. Just needs a sleep," she heard her father reply as she hurried upstairs to her room.

Susan pulled the crystal from her pocket and looked at it carefully.

"Crystal, are you doing this?" she asked.

The crystal lay still in her hand, but she felt peculiar. *I think I'll get ready as though I'm going on a crystal journey,* she thought.

Quickly she climbed into a long skirt and a blouse. She pulled on a large sweater and a jacket over that. She put on a pair of good solid runners that she had deliberately made black. All the time she was getting ready she could feel herself becoming less and less connected to the present and her room and her home. Chanting filled her ears, low, insistent, on and on.

This feels very strange, she thought. *I feel stretched.* The crystal tucked safe in a pocket of her skirt, she reached out to grab the large bag Mrs. Coleman had given her, the bag that contained all the things needed for a crystal journey. Before her hands could close on the handle, though, Susan's last slender contact with the present evaporated, and she felt herself moving, falling, tumbling, into no-when.

"Oh, this doesn't feel right at all." Susan's words were sucked away as she whirled on. *This is not how it felt when I went to help Jeremy,* she thought. *And it's going on a lot longer than it did before,* she added to herself. *What can be happening?*

Susan tumbled end over end. The chanting got louder. *This is so different from my other crystal journeys.*

She reached into her pocket and pulled out her crystal. The tumbling made her feel queasy and disoriented. She focused her attention on the crystal. She pinched it in her fingers and felt less buffeted by the tumbling and movement going on around her. She kept her eyes determinedly on the crystal. The chanting became louder still. Now she heard a stick beating a rhythm, too.

When is this going to end? she wondered.

Was her crystal smaller? Susan blinked. She looked again. Yes, smaller. The rhythm of the stick got faster. The chanting louder.

"Oh no, wait," she called. But it was too late; her crystal dwindled away to nothing in her fingers.

CHAPTER 4

WHERE AM I?

The rhythm and chanting stopped.
Silence.
Splash.

Susan landed on all fours in shallow water. Pain. Something hard and sharp dug into her hand. Oozy mud squished up through her fingers. It was night, dark and quiet. Instinctively, Susan's hand gripped the hard, sharp object. It came out of the ooze with a sucking sound. Not her crystal. She held a green rock about the size of her fist. She gripped it hard.

"Crystal," she called, standing up. "Crystal, I need you *now*." Susan held out her hand, but the Crystal of the North did not appear.

"Crystal, you are mine. Come now. I need you." She waited, but the crystal did not appear.

"*Crystal*," she called as loud as she could.

Nothing.

Susan stood, wet and shivering, gripping the green rock in her fist.

Then, in the quiet, the noises started. Susan first heard water gurgling, then frogs croaking, and then lots of unidentified rustling sounds. Susan shuddered. *I must be in a lake or river.* The water reached up to her knees. She tasted it. Fresh. Her feet sunk farther into the ooze. Susan pulled to get her feet free.

A gust of warm wind rippled across the water, making the nearby reeds rattle. Where was she?

In the starlight Susan saw only water and tall reeds. She turned full circle and saw no land anywhere.

Far away she noticed a bobbing light, then another, then another. They were low to the water and coming toward her. Rescue.

"Hello, I'm over here," she called.

It was obvious that someone had heard her. Voices came closer—calling.

Susan strained toward the advancing lights, trying to make out detail. She counted ten boats. Each carried three people. The light came from burning torches held high by a person standing in the prow. The central figure in each boat paddled.

The third passenger carried a shield and a spear. Soldier. Not like the soldiers Susan watched on television, but still a soldier. They wore helmets that shone in the torchlight.

Susan shrank back into the reeds. She shivered. She tried to pull more reeds over her head for cover. She lay very still. The boats drew nearer, quietly paddling through the ruffled water. From her hiding place, Susan heard the men talking back and forth between the boats. She couldn't understand a word they said.

Great, thought Susan, *the crystal has dragged me here—wherever here is—to help someone, whoever that is, and then disappeared. I've only got a lump of rock—and I can't even speak the language.*

At least it's warm, she realized. Even soaked through, she wasn't shivering from cold. Oh no. Now she shivered from fear.

The boats came closer. Susan breathed as quietly as she could. All the frogs and crickets went totally quiet as the boats approached. Every sound seemed magnified across the water. The boats moved around all the reed patches. One boat paddled right up to her reed bed, and a soldier peered in. He seemed to be looking right at her. Susan held her breath and stayed motionless. She could hear everything. She heard his spear sweeping through the reeds over her head. She heard the paddle dip into the water and the dribbles as it pulled out again. The torch crackled softly as it burned. She stayed frozen.

Like a deer in the forest, she thought.

Susan saw one of the men thrust his torch into the reeds. She watched, fascinated, as a curl of smoke drifted up. Too damp to burn fiercely, the reeds smoldered, sending up clouds of choking smoke. In minutes Susan was enveloped. She pulled a fold of her wet skirt around her mouth and nose.

No use. Coughing and spluttering and with her eyes running red, she struggled out of the reeds.

She stood in the water surrounded by the boats. Ten spears pointed at her chest.

CHAPTER 5

A ROCK AND A FEATHER

One soldier jumped into the water and grabbed her by the shirt. He was wearing a strip of white cloth wrapped around his middle. Around his neck he wore a necklace of beads with a medallion shaped like an eye hanging from it. He was short and lithe and tan.

Someone thrust a torch close to Susan's face, and she could hear them talking back and forth. They seemed puzzled and surprised. One made a comment, and the others all laughed.

Susan stood quietly, hoping that the soldier's grip on her shoulder would ease. Maybe she could hit him with her rock and make off into the darkness. The plan sounded desperate—even to her.

Apparently some decision had been made because the soldier holding her shrugged and lifted her into the closest boat. The boat rocked crazily under her sudden weight, and the soldier behind put a hand out and steadied her. She sat down quickly, and the little flotilla set off, skimming over the water.

The reeds on either side of the boat rose high, and so the boats seemed to be threading their way through watery corridors. When the person in the front of her boat dipped his torch into the water to extinguish it, Susan realized she could see without the torchlight. She looked up. Yes, the sky was lighter. Dawn.

Susan noticed that she was traveling in a reed boat. She felt the ridges against her feet where she sat cross-legged. As the paddler thrust with his oar, she could feel the reeds flexing against one another.

The boat was higher in the front and back but sank low into the water in the middle. As the sky grew lighter, she saw that the reeds were tied together with rope.

I'm glad I can swim, she thought.

Shortly, the boat thrust out of the reed beds, startling a flock of ducks into the air. They rose, protesting, flapping and noisy. Susan watched them fly. A falcon stooped out of the blue, talons outstretched, and grabbed one of the ducks. With a great squawk, the duck thrashed its wings about, but the falcon held on and soon flew away, clutching his prize.

One feather drifted down, swinging in the air currents. Susan reached out her hand, and it settled gently there. This caused a flurry of conversation between the boats. They drew closer together, and Susan could see the men looking at her sideways as they paddled past.

Susan looked at her prize. The feather stretched the length of her hand. There was a downy tuft at one end, and brown and white stripes stretched along the shaft. It felt good in Susan's hand.

Now I have two things, Susan thought as she smoothed the feather through her fingers.

The sun broke over the edge of the hills in the east. It was like someone had turned on a floodlight, bright and startling. First, one man began to sing in a loud clear voice. Soon others joined in, until most of the men were singing to the new day.

It sounds like a hymn, Susan thought.

Susan could see that they were on a wide river and paddling strongly for the eastern shore. She could see a strip of green along the riverbank and, in the hazy distance, pale reddish-colored hills. The town she could see looked most unusual. It seemed to have a wall built around it. Susan could only see the rooftops. Not like rooftops at home, though. Here the roofs were all flat, and she saw laundry spread to dry. In a few places people were walking around or sitting under awnings. On the roof.

All that living on the roof, Susan thought. *I wonder why there's a wall around the town.*

The boats skimmed toward the shore and soon entered the shelter of palm trees growing in the water.

This is odd, she thought. *It looks as though the river is flooded.*

It was eerie paddling among the palms. Their leaves clicked in the slight dawn breeze blowing up the river.

The boat cleared the last of the palms, and Susan's boat bumped against a reed raft that floated on the water. The soldier jumped out first. The other two men held the boat to the raft. The soldier lifted Susan out and carefully set her on her feet.

Pins and needles. She had been sitting too long. She stumbled and almost fell, but the soldier grasped her elbow and held her up. She stamped her feet to get the blood flowing again, and the soldier waited patiently until she was ready.

Then the soldiers formed up around her and politely invited her to march along with them.

I don't know where else they think I was going, she thought as she hurried to keep up. *I've got a rock and a feather and a very wet skirt to my name—and no crystal.*

Susan almost panicked, and she stumbled. *How will I get home?*

She took a deep breath and straightened. *Suck it up, Susan. No good getting in a dither. You'll just have to work it out.*

A rope and a walkway, also made of reed bundles, tethered the floating raft to the shore. It bounced perilously as they marched across it. They passed through a door in a blank wall and came out into a lovely garden.

There was no time to admire the flowers, though, because they hustled her across the grass, through a doorway, and into a large building.

They left her. Susan stood in a courtyard. Behind her was the door, and on the other three sides, archways led into shaded walkways. She saw doorways through the walkways, and most of the soldiers disappeared through one of these. She heard talking and laughter and then silence and scuffling. Faces appeared in the doorways. People quietly stared at her.

As she stood in the courtyard, the first rays of the morning sun reached over the wall. The heat rose up around her. *My skirt is already dry*, Susan noticed. She shuffled across the courtyard until she was standing in the shade.

Presently, one of the soldiers returned. He surprised her by bowing. When he pulled her gently by the arm, she followed him.

He led her to a workroom.

CHAPTER 6
THE MAGICIAN

Susan stood just inside the door. A long, wide bench built out from the wall stretched along one wall. Pots and jars and a couple of metal pans rested on the bench, and in one corner, a metal container had a fire burning inside it. Suspended over the fire was a large pot, which bubbled. Green vapor drifted in the air above the pot.

Shelves occupied all the available wall space. These were cluttered with ceramic pots of all shapes and sizes. Some had funny writing on the sides.

The wall above the workbench didn't reach to the roof. Light flooded into the room through the narrow gap.

It's not a window, thought Susan. *There's no glass, and you can't see out.*

The man working at the bench turned around and marched straight up to her.

He thrust his face close to hers and spoke sharply to her.

It sounded like gibberish to Susan. She shrugged.

"Where am I?" Susan asked him.

The man frowned and said the same thing to her in a louder voice.

"Where am I?" Susan yelled back.

The man took her by the shoulders and shook her, saying the same thing over and over.

Susan stamped on his bare foot.

The man jumped back and glared at her.

Susan glared back. *I hope I look more fierce than I feel,* she thought.

The soldier moved forward and began talking rapidly. He moved his hands as he spoke and Susan watched closely.

First the soldier told about Susan coughing as she moved out of the rushes. He put his hand up to his mouth and pretended to cough, and moved his hands to show how the smoke billowed out of the rushes. Then he held his hand up menacingly as though he had a rock in it.

I hope I looked that unafraid, Susan thought as she saw her story unfold.

Susan watched as the soldier continued the story. Lastly, she saw him swoop his hands.

He's telling about the hawk. She could see.

Then Susan watched as the soldier told about the feather drifting down. He held his hand out, as she had done, and he showed the feather resting on her hand as he finished talking.

He never showed me as afraid, or crying, or upset. I think the soldier thinks I'm brave, Susan realized.

The man took a step back and looked at her with his head on one side.

Just like Mum looking at her sculpture, Susan thought with a pang.

Quickly the man went to his bench. He pulled out a couple of sticks and began rapidly rolling the paper attached to them, back and forth.

It's a scroll, Susan realized. *I saw a scroll on a television show. Maybe I'm in ancient Greece.*

Finally he found the writing he was looking for. He read for a moment and then pulled a large pan from a shelf.

Quickly he began moving along the shelves, muttering and mumbling to himself as he went. He pulled down several pots and poured measures of their contents into his pan. With much consulting of his scroll and smelling of his pots, he finally began stirring his concoction.

I don't think that's breakfast, Susan thought. Her stomach rumbled.

Once he'd put the pan over his little fire, the room began to fill with a horrible smell. He didn't seem to notice but began singing in a humdrum drone.

That's the sort of chanting I heard when I was being pulled here. Is this guy responsible for me being here without my crystal? I wish I'd stamped on his foot harder.

Holding her nose and looking around, Susan saw a low bench against the back wall. She moved over to it and sat down. She was bone weary.

She watched the man. Smaller than her father but about the same age. He wore a white kilt similar to the soldier's. His was of a much finer material, though. It was almost sheer. A belt held it up. A belt studded with bright patches of color, as though pretty stones had been stuck to the leather. The belt was knotted over and fell in elaborate folds down the front of the kilt.

Around his neck he wore a collar of colored beads, which reached out to the width of his shoulders and down onto his chest.

His head was completely bald.

He bent over the mixture and then twinkled his fingers in a complicated gesture over the bowl.

That seemed to finish his potion because he carefully poured half of it into a cup. And then he advanced toward Susan.

She stood.

"Oh no," she said, shaking her head. "Not in this lifetime."

The man grabbed her neck and held the cup close to her mouth. She clamped her jaw shut and shook her head hard from side to side.

The man made a signal, and the soldier grabbed her shoulders, holding her steady. Susan kept struggling. She kicked out, but the soldier held her tight. The man grabbed her nose and squeezed it hard. She could feel her face swell; she held her breath; her eyes bugged out. It was no good; she had to breathe. She opened her mouth and down the awful mixture went.

Susan tried to spit, but he held her jaw shut and she had to swallow to breathe.

"That's disgusting," she said as soon as she stopped coughing and spluttering.

That's what she said—but not what she heard.

It came out as something else.

"Stop struggling, you little fool. You're not hurt." She could understand what the man said to her.

Amazing.

Susan tried again. "Where am I? Who are you?"

The man didn't answer. He peered right in her face. His expression said plainly that he was not impressed. Susan stood her ground.

"You're not a magician," he accused. "I conjured a magician, and I got you."

"Then send me back," Susan snapped.

The man ignored her.

He turned and picked up the bowl with the other half of the mixture. Susan braced herself for a fight; she wasn't drinking any more of that stuff. But the man poured the rest carefully into the other pan, still simmering over the fire.

"Yes, yes," Susan heard him muttering as he stirred it in. "I've solved the problem of language. Who would have expected that they wouldn't speak our language? Any educated magician should know the civilized language." He glared at Susan over his shoulder. "What a barbarian." He sniffed.

Barbarian? Now Susan was sure that this man was from her past, and she was sure that even though she was only ten, she knew things he did not. She had to think hard against the new language. She screwed her face up with concentration. What did she know that he didn't?

"Television, cell phone, spaceship, 747, F18, satellite, Internet," she said in a rush.

As an afterthought she wiggled her fingers in the air as she had seen him do.

The magician turned to her with a look of astonishment on his face. "Those are powerful words," he said. "What do they mean?"

"They're my magic," Susan said and tried to look down her nose at him.

"The numbers sound like a special formula," he said with a question in his voice.

Oops, numbers will translate into the new language, Susan realized.

"Yes," she said, "people can fly when they use those numbers correctly."

The magician looked very impressed. "Ah, daughter." The man actually bowed to her. "You are welcome in the home of Harsheer, Beloved of Pharaoh, Mighty in the Service of Amen-Re, Protector of the Royal Tomb." He bowed again, holding his hand to his chest.

Unsure what to do, Susan bowed back.

Harsheer laid his hand on the top of her head.

"Merit-Amen," he said. "I will call you Merit-Amen, princess—daughter of my house. I adopt you."

Susan's mouthed dropped open. "Just like that, I'm a princess?"

"You are my daughter." Harsheer waggled his fingers. "We'll worry about the other titles later."

Susan slumped back onto the bench.

"Go and get cleaned up. You look so...uncivilized." Harsheer made shooing motions for her to leave the room.

Susan stood, and the soldier gently took her arm and guided her out. Looking back into the room as the door shut behind them, Susan saw Harsheer, already absorbed in the work at his bench again.

CHAPTER 7

LOOKING CIVILIZED!

The soldier guided Susan along a passage. Susan went where she was tugged. She didn't want to think about anything. They followed the smell of onions and soon arrived in an open courtyard.

Some of the soldiers and paddlers were clustered around a small cooking fire set in one corner. They were talking excitedly with a small group of women. From their hand gestures Susan saw they were talking about her.

One of the women squeaked when she noticed Susan walking toward them. They all stopped talking and turned to stare at her.

"Meet Princess Merit-Amen," the soldier escorting her announced in a loud voice. "She is the daughter of this house," he added, flourishing his arm in Susan's direction.

How embarrassing, thought Susan, trying to smooth her rumpled, muddy skirt.

She heard the people whispering, and when she looked up, she saw surprise in most of their faces. One woman stepped forward.

"I am Nozme," she said. "Welcome."

Susan bowed. "Thank you," she said.

A girl not much older than Susan came pushing through the crowd. She carried a large platter across her two arms. She bowed low to Susan.

"Princess Merit-Amen, are you hungry?" she asked.

At the sight of the food, Susan's stomach rumbled. She nodded and reached for a drumstick from the platter. It smelled wonderful. She bit into it.

Not exactly like chicken. Susan sighed, it tasted so good.

"Thank you," she said, chewing as fast as she could.

Nozme turned to the girl and waved her hand. "This is Teo," she said. "Teo, bring a napkin for the princess," she ordered.

Teo ran off to get a napkin, and everyone else just stared.

Susan quickly ate another drumstick.

Nozme finally turned to the soldier. "Hori, what are we supposed to do with her?" she asked.

Well, I know what I want, Susan decided.

"I would like a bath and some clean clothes," she said, trying to sound like a princess—however that was.

"Oh, of course." Nozme moved quickly. "Of course, you need everything."

Hori piped up. "Harsheer, who is the magician, said to make her look civilized."

Several people sniggered behind their hands.

Nozme glared them into silence. Teo arrived back with a napkin, and Susan used it to mop her face and hide her embarrassment.

Nozme barked some short, sharp orders.

"Come." Nozme gently took Susan by the shoulder and pushed her toward the passageway again. A troupe of people followed, carrying jars of steaming water and chests and boxes.

They entered a room that seemed set aside for bathing. The floor was set with stones, and in one corner was a small tub carved from stone. The people began pouring warm water into this tub, and Nozme added some oil from a jar. A wonderful smell of flowers wafted from the water into the room. Susan felt better already.

Under Nozme's direction, the boxes and chests were set against the wall, and soon just Susan, Nozme, and Teo were left in the little room.

"Come now, Princess, in you get." Nozme waved toward the tub.

Susan would rather have her bath in private, but it didn't seem that these two were going to leave and she couldn't see the soap, so Susan slipped quickly out of her clothes and into the scented warm water.

Teo went over to the pile of clothes that Susan had dropped and began picking up each piece and examining it. She seemed surprised to see so many pieces. Susan, watching, noticed that both Nozme and Teo were wearing just a simple one-piece dress.

Just a tube of material really, she thought as she looked more closely at their dresses. Then Nozme began to rub her back with a soft cloth. It felt so good.

Susan was tired, and now she felt so comfortable and relaxed that she drowsed. The gentle rubbing of the cloth over her limbs soothed her. It was quiet in the little room. Nozme began rubbing her head. Susan sighed and slipped even further into her doze.

Susan was never sure how long she drifted close to sleep, but the next thing she was conscious of was a vague scraping feeling over her head. It felt quite pleasant so she took little notice. The scraping continued, and then Nozme took her head in her hands and moved it decisively to the other side.

Susan opened one eye to see what was happening. Her hair was floating in the water. Flick. As she watched, another swatch of her wet hair landed in the water. Her hair?

Susan was awake now, and on her feet. She quickly ran her hand over her scalp. Her hair was gone. There was just one hank of hair hanging on the right side; otherwise she was as bald as an egg.

"What have you done to me?" she yelled. "My hair, my hair." She jumped out of the tub.

Nozme looked surprised. She shook her head. Teo squealed and began to bawl loudly.

"Shut up," Susan and Nozme yelled at Teo together and then turned on each other.

"I liked my hair. How dare you cut it off," Susan yelled, hands on hips.

"I was told to make you look civilized, you little barbarian," Nozme yelled back, bringing her nose very close to Susan's.

"Civilized, civilized, bald is civilized?" Susan's voice rose higher and higher. She was so angry.

Teo bawled louder, wailing in fright.

"I left you a youth lock, what are you complaining about?" Nozme snapped.

"I'll look stupid, stupid. Ugly, ugly. Where's my hair," Susan wailed. She was so angry she trembled.

There were scuffling noises and whispering in the corridor outside the door.

Nozme advanced on her. "You are stupid. A stupid little girl." Nozme grabbed her by the arms. "You couldn't go out looking like a barbarian. You're a princess now. Act like one," she whispered, looking over her shoulder to the door.

Susan's pulled to get away from Nozme's grasp. She reached out to brace herself, and her hand caught in Nozme's hair. It moved. Susan pulled. Nozme's hair came off in her hands. Nozme was bald, and Susan was holding her wig, clutched in her hands.

They both stopped and stood, too surprised to move.

Teo let out another wail from the corner where she was huddling.

"Be quiet," Susan and Nozme both snapped at her at the same time.

Teo gulped. Susan and Nozme caught each other's eye, and then the storm was over. Suddenly it all just seemed too funny. Susan reached up and tried to set the wig back on Nozme's head. It hung there crookedly. And then they were both laughing.

Feeling calmer, Susan had time to notice things again. *I'm wet from the bath but not cold.* Nozme handed her a cloth, and she began to dry herself.

The routine actions of drying herself helped her to calm. The cloth Nozme gave her wasn't nobby like the towels she was used to, but as she rubbed it over her arm she saw that it was soaking up the beads of moisture from her skin. Such a familiar thing was a comfort when her surroundings and circumstances were anything but ordinary.

I'm alive. I have had something to eat. I'm in a house. I'm a princess. Susan chuckled to herself. *What could possibly happen next?*

Nozme straightened her wig, and Susan had an opportunity to study her. Nozme looked about the same age as her mother, although she seemed a lot shorter than Alice Sinclair. Her eyes were brown and her skin tanned to a lovely, deep brown. She was slim and lithe. She looked strong and yet dainty.

Nozme looks like a pretty interesting person, Susan thought.

Teo, still sniffling to herself, busily pulled pots and jars from the boxes and arranged them on a shelf. Teo seemed just a couple of years older than Susan and was actually smaller. Her hair was black. *I wonder if that's a wig, too.* Teo set down a tall blue pot, and it tipped over. Teo squeaked and looked around to see if anyone had noticed. *She seems pretty timid,* Susan observed.

Nozme picked up one of the jars and poured the contents into her hands. A sweet smell of flowers filled the room. She began rubbing the stuff into Susan's arms. It was a kind of oil. *Like suntan oil,* she thought.

"Why do you shave your heads?" Susan asked.

Nozme shrugged. "That's just the way it is," she said.

"Are you going to shave off this other bit, too?" Susan asked, flipping the hank of hair left on the side of her head.

"No." Nozme shook her head. "That's a youth lock. All the children your age wear their hair like that."

"When I go home, everyone will laugh at me," Susan said, more to herself than to Nozme.

"Oh, this is your home now. He made you the daughter of the house," Nozme declared, pulling Susan to her feet.

Teo held another cloth. This one of sheer gauzy material. Nozme draped it around Susan's waist and used a clip to hold it. Susan was wearing a short white wrap-around skirt that reached just to her knees.

"Come," said Nozme. "It's almost time for the afternoon rest. Teo will take you to the room we have prepared for you, and I will bring you a plate of food."

"Wait," Susan hesitated. "Where are the rest of my clothes?"

"Oh, we took them away. They're no good for our country. You have to look like a civilized person now."

"No"—Susan waved at the little skirt she was wearing—"where are the rest of my clothes for here?"

"You're wearing your clothes." Nozme frowned. "You don't want to put on your jewelry and paint your face before sleeping. We'll do that when you wake up." Nozme began to herd her toward the door.

"I can't go out there in just this skirt." Susan dug in her heels.

"Yes, you can," insisted Nozme and thrust her through the doorway into the corridor.

CHAPTER 8

A BREATHING SPACE

Susan lay quietly on a high, uncomfortable bed. Instead of a pillow, her head was perched on a hard stand and the bed sloped so that her head was higher than her feet. *It's like trying to sleep on the side of a hill*, she thought, as she tried to make sense of all that had happened to her.

Her head prickled where it was shaved, and the skin felt tight. Susan ran her hand over her bald head. What would her parents say? *That's if I ever get home again*, Susan worried. *Crystal, where are you? Why am I here? Who am I supposed to help?* Susan held out her hand and willed her crystal to come. But it did not.

Susan felt hot and sticky. She had never been anywhere so hot in her life.

The sun blazed into the room from the high windows. Even with the slatted blinds pulled over the openings, Susan could feel the heat. She slipped quietly off the bed and crept across the room. A small mirror, made of polished metal, stood on a chest against the far wall.

How round her head was. Susan turned sideways to see the lock of hair she had left. A slow tear trickled down her cheek.

She brushed it away angrily and turned away from the mirror. The tears blurring her eyes caused her to stub her toe on the chest beside her bed. The lid flipped open, and she looked in. There lay her green stone and the falcon feather. *I have two things to my name.* She sighed.

Lying again on the uncomfortable bed, Susan eventually fell asleep.

>—<+>—<

She awakened to the sound of Teo opening the window blinds.

"Magician Harsheer is calling for you, Princess."

CHAPTER 9

PRINCESS
MERIT-AMEN—OR?

Susan sprang up from the funny bed. The air felt cooler. *Maybe now I'll get some answers,* she hoped. She smoothed down her sheath and started for the door.

"Wait, wait," Teo called. "You can't appear before the master looking like that."

Before Susan could reply, Nozme bustled into the room, her hands full of boxes and bundles.

"The magician Harsheer has opened his treasury to you," she said, turning Susan toward a stool. "Sit. We must try to make you look civilized." Nozme turned Susan's head critically from side to side. "And like a princess," she added.

"We'll start with the oil." Nozme held her hands out to Teo, who passed her a beautifully shaped bottle. "Not that one," Nozme snapped. "Merit-Amen is a princess. Bring me the myrrh."

Teo hurried out and returned with a small, delicate little bottle. She was sniffing again and wiping at tears on her face.

Nozme rubbed the oil all over Susan's body. Even her poor bald head got the treatment. It helped with the itching.

"Take this sheath," said Nozme, handing Susan a fresh white piece of material. The material was twirled around itself, and when Susan shook it out, the material showed pleats. *Like a broomstick skirt,* thought Susan. She could see right through the fine material. There were little beads of blue and red stitched around the hem. Two straps over her shoulders held the dress up.

Out of the chests and boxes, Nozme pulled heavy bracelets and draped them on Susan's wrists and ankles. Next Nozme pulled out ornate dangles and hung them in Susan's ears.

Thank goodness I had my ears pierced last year, Susan thought. She peered at herself in the "look-face," the name Nozme gave to the polished metal mirror.

Next they settled a wide collar of woven beads around her throat. The collar reached the width of her shoulders and was made of small blue, red, and green beads strung into patterns on copper wire.

Then they combed and oiled her remaining tuft of hair. Teo helped Nozme string tiny beads onto some hair strands, and then they plaited it tightly. The braid fell to just below Susan's ear. Teo tied small silver bells onto the end of the braid. Susan moved her head, and the bells tinkled. As she stood up, Susan caught a glimpse of herself in the look-face.

I look Egyptian, she thought.

"Is this Egypt?" Susan asked Nozme.

Teo immediately burst into loud bawling and wailing.

"Of course it is," Nozme answered and, taking Susan's arm, led her to where Magician Harsheer waited.

At the edge of the garden, Nozme gave Susan a little push and then turned and walked back inside. Susan walked on alone.

Nozme had given her no shoes to wear, and Susan was not used to walking barefoot. She could feel every pebble and every blade of grass beneath her feet.

Harsheer lay under a shady tree beside a large pond. As Susan approached, she saw flowers floating in the water. The garden had a cool, fresh smell, with the sweetness of many flowers and an overall smell of soft honey. She heard bees droning through the flowers as she walked past.

I wonder if I should bow, Susan thought as she approached.

In her bare feet, she made no sound and so she could watch Harsheer as she approached. He seemed a million miles away. Then he turned sharply toward her, as though he sensed her approach.

"There you are at last," he snapped. He looked her up and down coolly. "Looking civilized, I see."

Susan bobbed her knees—it seemed the appropriate thing to do.

"Sit, sit," Harsheer ordered, gesturing to the cushion next to him.

"Is this Egypt?" Susan blurted out.

"Of course," Harsheer replied. "This is the wonderful land of Egypt. I am a mighty prince of Egypt. The great pharaoh Akheperenre has honored me and made me High Priest and Reader, Master Magician to His Mighty Person, and Keeper and Protector of His Tomb."

"When is this Egypt?" was all Susan wanted to know.

"I'll tell you my other titles later," Harsheer said with a wave of his hand. "You'll have to learn them all before we reach Thebes. Now, let's see…" He began muttering to himself as though alone. Susan heard words like *inundation* and *travel* and *mystery* and *formula*.

Susan's attention was drawn to two ducks diving in the pond. Heads up, and then tails up as they searched for dinner. It was pleasant by the pond. It was cool, and a soft breeze blew through the garden. But her attention suddenly flashed back on Harsheer because in his muttering he had said *crystal*. That was a subject that really interested Susan.

"What about crystals?" Susan asked sharply.

"Don't you listen to anything?" Harsheer retorted. "I brought you here to help me make Ma'at's crystals."

"How do you mean, you brought me here? I thought my crystal was responsible."

Harsheer quirked his eyebrow. "You already have a crystal?"

"Yes, I am the Guardian of the Crystal of the North, and it takes me on journeys to where I am needed."

Harsheer sat up straight and puffed out his chest. "I brought you here. I wove the spells to draw you to me."

"You dragged me here?" Susan's voice was rising angrily. *That explains why the journey felt different.*

"I conjured a great crystal magician to assist me in making the most wonderful crystals in the world."

"I wouldn't assist you to make an omelet, you… you time-napper, you."

Harsheer fell back on his pillows in the face of Susan's anger.

"Give me back my crystal and send me home immediately." Susan sprang to her feet, too angry to sit still another minute. "I don't want to be a princess— I want to be Susan Sinclair. I already have a crystal and don't need to help you make more. Now send me home immediately."

Harsheer sprang to his feet as well. He towered over her.

"It took three months to conjure the spell to bring you here. Three months of my precious time. You will help me if you ever want to get home. I don't have your crystal. Work with me to conjure my crystals, and I'll give you one."

"I won't help you. How dare you drag me across time without asking." Susan crossed her arms across her chest and planted her feet. She put on her most stubborn face. "And besides," she added, "my crystal isn't just any crystal. It's very special."

"I'll give you three reasons why you will do as you're told." Harsheer towered over her threateningly. "Sun, toil, food."

"I suppose that's supposed to scare me," Susan retorted.

"It should," Harsheer answered, looking more confident now. "If you don't help me, I'll turn you out. Where will you go? What will you eat? How will you get home then?"

Susan dropped to the grass. She stayed still. *This can't be happening to me.* But it was happening, and she was alone in a very strange place. Susan sucked in a sobbing breath. She was too angry to speak; she looked up and glared at Harsheer—and faintly nodded. "All right, I'll help you," she said.

Harsheer bent down and patted her shoulder, looking pleased with himself. "That's more like it," he said. "Come along. Let's get started."

Susan rose and followed Harsheer to his workroom. *I'll not forget this*, she thought. *I can't trust this Harsheer, not for a minute.*

CHAPTER 10
BEFORE THE CRYSTAL

"What does your crystal look like?" Harsheer asked as he rummaged on his table among the scrolls.

It was hard to describe, and Susan held up her fingers to try to show the size and shape of it.

"Like this?" Harsheer asked and thrust a piece of papyrus under her nose.

All the wind puffed out of Susan. The ancient scroll showed an exact drawing of her crystal. She touched the picture gently with her finger.

"Exactly," was all she could say.

"Hmm." Harsheer rubbed his bald head with his hand. It made a soft, scratchy sound.

"Now I see," he added and began rummaging among the pots on his table.

"See what?" Susan asked.

With a sigh of impatience, Harsheer turned to her. With a look of irritation on his face and his hands on his hips, he said, "Well, of course, that's why your crystal shrank and disappeared—in this time it's not made yet."

"Not made yet?" Susan couldn't fathom what he was talking about.

Harsheer waved an airy hand at the jumble on the work table and then bent and blew on the little fire under his bubbling pot. When he had the fire glowing, he turned to Susan again.

"Yes, of course, it makes sense. I called you here to help me make the Four Crystals of Ma'at. They will be of great power. In your own time you obviously possessed one of them and now you're here. You will help me make them."

Harsheer took a deep breath and struck a pose. "I'll be famous throughout the two lands. Maybe I'll become a god."

Maybe he'll get eaten by a crocodile, Susan thought, amused at his posturing. *Oh, maybe that's why the paper at home was blank when I looked at it. I'm in a time before my crystal was created. Huh.* And then she thought further. *I have to help this puffed up guy or the crystals may never be made.*

"I've got the scroll here." Harsheer interrupted her thoughts. "We'll make the four of them, and then you can take the one you want, and I'll have the other three. Then you can go home."

"But, but...what if we can't make the crystal, I'll be stuck here."

"Oh, don't worry." Harsheer waved his hand again. "Now that you're here, I'm sure it will work this time."

"How many times have you tried?" Susan asked doubtfully.

"Oh, don't worry about it. They were just practices," Harsheer said spreading the scroll across the table. "I have you now. The tenth time is lucky, they say."

"Ten times you've tried." Susan felt faint and slumped onto the bench.

Harsheer hardly noticed her upset, he was so absorbed in his pan and fire and scroll. Once he had everything bubbling to his satisfaction, he brought the scroll over to where Susan was slumped.

"See," he said, holding the scroll up to her, "there was a fold in the scroll, and I didn't notice it in the beginning. Inside the folded bit was the instructions for summoning a powerful crystal magician to add power to the spell to make the crystals."

Susan looked at the scroll. It was covered with squiggles and lines that meant nothing to her. *I may be able to speak the language, but I can't read it,* she realized. She saw the creases in the scroll, though, and within the creases there was quite a lot of writing and a picture of a little statue.

She pointed to the picture. "What is that?" she asked.

"Ah." Harsheer puffed his chest with pride. "That's a statuette I made to summon you. The writing tells me how."

"So," asked Susan. "That little statue has the power to drag me away from my home. Can't it send me back as well?"

Harsheer jumped up nervously. "Um, of course not. It's only one way." He rolled the scroll tightly in his hands and hurried over to the table.

Susan followed close behind, but she missed what he rummaged for on the table before she got there.

He turned quickly with his hands behind his back. "You'll help me make the crystals, and then you can go back."

Susan was certain he was hiding something.

Nozme entered, carrying a tray laden with food, and Susan realized how hungry she was. *Well, I'll have to keep my strength up to get through this adventure,* she thought, and hurried over to take a plate.

Harsheer came over, too. "Nozme," he said, "inform everyone we leave for Thebes tomorrow morning early."

"It's mostly all arranged," Nozme replied. "You'll almost be too late as it is."

"Nevertheless, we will stop to inspect the royal tomb on the way," Harsheer said. "Make sure all Princess Merit-Amen's things are ready in plenty of time."

Nozme left, shaking her head.

Susan chewed slowly. There were no knives and forks so she had to eat with her fingers. She picked up the pieces of meat and tried to put them into her mouth without dripping juice on her chin. The bread was easier, and she broke off pieces and ate them slowly. She watched Harsheer dip his bread into a stew of onions and other vegetables, and so she tried that, too. Delicious. Harsheer threw her a napkin to wipe her chin.

"You have a lot to learn, and we have a lot to do before we reach the palace," he said.

CHAPTER 11

THE CRYSTAL FORMULA

For hours they worked together, mixing and boiling the ingredients for making the crystals. Harsheer hardly spoke except to grunt at her or give instructions about where to find different things on the shelves. He was annoyed that she couldn't read the squiggles on the jars.

"You'll have to go to school with the palace scribes when we get to Thebes," he said, shaking a wooden spoon in her face.

"Just send me home," Susan replied, holding her nose against the smell coming from the pot she stirred. "I read very well in my language."

Harsheer harrumphed and bent his head to the scroll again.

As she stirred Susan thought about her crystal and tried to remember everything Mrs. Coleman had told her about it. She remembered exactly how it looked and how it felt like a part of her, and then she remembered the times that it had surprised her by doing the unexpected.

She smiled at the thought of Jeremy's surprise when she arrived on the ship with a coat for him. Then a thought struck her. *Oh, if the crystal doesn't grow I won't be able to help Jeremy.* And that led to another thought. *What about all the people that Mrs. Coleman helped over the years. What will happen to them?* And then the thought got bigger. *There's going to be four crystals. That's four times the amount of helping people and balancing wrongs that won't happen in the world if I don't help this weird magician grow these crystals. They must be exactly right.* Susan shook her head. *All those people who need us crystal guardians to set things right. The world would be a different place without our crystals. Maybe there wouldn't even be an internet.*

"Harsheer, can we make the crystal more reliable? So that it will do exactly what its Guardian wants?" Susan asked.

Harsheer cocked his head to one side, thinking. "It should be possible, but we would need more time."

"Well, how long? A few more days wouldn't matter to get it right." *I can always time it to arrive during the night that I left,* Susan knew.

"A few days." Harsheer laughed. "A few years more like. It would take three inundations to make it absolutely reliable."

Susan said nothing. She went on stirring, but her brain was racing. Three inundations sounded like a long time.

Finally she plucked up the courage to ask, "How long is it going to take to grow these crystals?"

Harsheer, deep in thought, waggled his fingers at her. "Six months."

Six months. Susan's heart sank. Six months living with this puffed-up person in this strange, hot place. Six months. She kept on stirring. What else was there for her to do? *What if he doesn't get it right the first time?* she thought. *I could look older by the time I get home.*

Susan realized she would do anything to make the crystals grow properly the first time. So much depended on it.

Finally Harsheer said the potion was ready. They had added hundreds of ingredients to the pot, which had already been bubbling when Susan arrived. She had no idea what was in there. She spent half the night grinding and pounding and stirring.

Susan peered over the rim of the pan. The mixture was a brownish, yellowish, greenish liquid in the bottom; the smell wasn't so much a smell as something that grabbed her nose and made it run. Susan's eyes watered. Her face was reflected in the still surface. As she looked, she thought she saw lights dancing within the liquid.

Suddenly Harsheer grabbed her hand and thrust it into the pot. It was hot. Susan struggled.

"Be still," Harsheer whispered in her ear. "This is the hard part."

With their two hands thrust into the liquid, Harsheer had her repeat phrases from the scroll. She said the words carefully, as they meant nothing to her. Some of the words sounded like this new language she had learned, but even then they were different.

I think this is very old Egyptian, she thought as she mumbled on.

Finally Harsheer lifted his hand from the pot, and Susan did the same. The liquid slid off her skin. Her hand was completely dry, and there was no ripple on the surface of the liquid.

"Stand back," Harsheer ordered and carefully poured the contents from the pan into a stone flask. The walls of the flask were so fine that Susan could see the liquid rising as Harsheer poured. *I wonder what sort of stone can be so strong and yet we can see through it.*

"The flask is carved from alabaster," Harsheer explained, as though he were proud to own such a rare and beautiful container. "It's very old."

Susan stepped wearily away. Her new sidelock felt heavy on her head. She flapped it to fan her face.

Susan's attention was caught by something small and black near Harsheer's feet. She peered closer and saw a little statue that looked exactly like the one in the scroll.

That's the statue Harsheer used to get me here. That statue gives him power over me, Susan realized. She glanced quickly at Harsheer. All his attention was focused on the liquid pouring slowly from the pan. She sidled up to the table, and while she pretended to be watching Harsheer, she kicked the statue under the bench out of sight.

"We must be certain that no air gets in to start the crystal forming before we get it to its growing place," Harsheer explained as he dripped candle wax over the seal.

"Where is that?" Susan asked.

"You'll see," Harsheer answered. "Now go to bed. We leave soon."

Susan stumbled as she turned toward the door. *I can't ever remember being this tired,* she thought as she walked down the central corridor, holding a tiny lamp in her hands.

CHAPTER 12

THE STATUETTE

As soon as Susan entered, Teo leaped to her feet and hurried over to help Susan out of her clothes. Teo's eyes were red in the lamplight, and she was sniffing back more tears.

Susan was so tired she plopped onto the stool and let Teo unfasten the bead collar she was wearing.

"Why do you cry all the time?" she asked.

"I'm far from my home, Princess," Teo answered, starting to cry softly again.

"I'm far from my home, too," Susan said, a little exasperated, "but crying isn't going to fix it and get me home any sooner."

"You're going home, mistress?" Teo asked, so surprised that she stopped crying in midsob.

"Well, not straight away, but, yes, I'm going home." Susan rubbed her shoulders where the collar had lain.

"I'll never go home," Teo said, and there was such sadness in her tone that Susan bit her lip and scratched her scalp.

"Why did Harsheer make me a princess?" Susan asked, hoping to distract Teo.

"Ah." Teo smiled a little through the tears. "In Thebes the mighty Magician Harsheer, boasted to the Great Pharaoh, Akheperenre, Father of the People, that he would summon a mighty magician to his estate. A mighty magician of great power who would help him weave wonderful magics for the court and make fools of all the pharaoh's enemies."

"Yes, but why did he make me a princess?" Susan asked again.

"Wait, Mistress, and I will tell you." Teo began unpicking the beads from Susan's sidelock as she talked. "He came here to his estate far from the city, and he worked day and night at a mighty conjuring. He mixed and brewed in his little room for days. Only Nozme was allowed to enter, and she only went in to take him food. He never slept. All hours of the day and night, we heard him singing and mumbling, calling on gods and whatever else. Then last night, we heard the loudest noise any of us had ever heard. It sounded as though every piece of linen in the two kingdoms tore at once. It sounded as though the desert had split in two. Then there was a mighty silence."

Susan sighed. "What happened?"

Teo shrugged. "Nothing."

"Yes, but why did he make me a princess?"

"Well, he had performed a huge summoning, and nobody came. He sent boats out onto the river, and he sent soldiers in chariots into the desert to find the mighty magician he had summoned. And…" Teo paused for effect. "They came back with you."

"And he had to make me a princess and somebody grand because if I was just an ordinary young girl, he would look stupid." Susan finished the story.

Teo nodded.

Susan walked over to her couch and lay down with a sigh. The silly thing was starting to feel comfortable. She was so tired.

"Good night, Teo." She pulled the flimsy covers up to her shoulders.

"Good night Princess," Teo answered, curling up on the floor.

Susan, was two breaths from sleep when she remembered the little statue in the workroom.

She sat up slowly on the bed. Teo didn't stir. She rose and groped for her discarded sheath. Teo didn't stir. She passed her hand over the chest, trying to feel for the little lamp that rested there. Her fingers knocked it against a pot, and it made a dull clunk.

Susan froze. Teo didn't stir. Susan tiptoed across the room as quietly as she could.

"Do you require assistance, Princess? Teo asked sleepily.

Susan started, then swallowed to get her voice even. "No, Teo, go to sleep," she whispered and crept out through the door. She encountered no one in the central passageway, but she could hear distant movement in the house as she hurried along to the workroom door.

She reached out to open it and then froze. *What if Harsheer is inside?*

Susan pressed her ear to the door. Nothing. Taking a deep breath, she quickly opened the door and slipped into the workroom. The entire room was a-dazzle with dancing lights. Susan had never seen such a display. Moving to the workbench, Susan caught sight of the sealed bottle that contained the crystal mixture. The lights started deep inside and shone out into the room.

In the dancing light, Susan knelt and groped under the bench for the statuette. It was still there. Susan sighed with relief as she snuggled the little figure of herself in her hand and tiptoed to the door.

She was reluctant to leave the wonderful lights but didn't want to be caught in the workroom.

Just as she reached the door, she heard footsteps outside.

Please let it be soldiers. Please let them be going past.

Susan heard every word they said.

"I tell you, she is powerful. Otherwise why would the falcon feather rest so readily in her hand?" said one soldier.

Hori answered, "The great god Horus has spread his protective wings over her, that's for sure."

Susan heard one of the soldiers trip.

"Careful with that," Hori muttered. "Grab your end and carry it carefully. Do you want to wake Harsheer?"

Susan couldn't imagine what they were doing and didn't care. She waited until they were gone and then stole carefully along the passage to her own door.

When she lay again in her own bed, she had time to wonder what the soldier had meant about Horus spreading his wings over her. Who was Horus? *I must make sure I keep that feather,* she thought.

Then she slept.

CHAPTER 13

ON THE RIVER

"But I just shut my eyes," Susan groaned as she awoke to Teo's shaking.

"Princess, quickly, the boat is waiting. We need to get down to the river." Teo kept shaking her as she spoke.

"OK, Teo, I'm awake." Susan sat up, rubbing the sleep from her eyes.

Two lamps lit the room. Bedding was rolled and tied, and all her chests and boxes were fastened and stacked by the door.

Teo handed her a fresh sheath with a bob of her head.

"I saved you this to wear, Princess," she said.

Without giving it a second thought, Susan whipped the skimpy sheath over her head and stretched. There was a morning chill in the air, and she shivered a little. Teo immediately handed her a beautiful cape of soft light wool. It folded around her shoulders and reached almost to her feet. A deep hood covered her bald head. Susan felt a pocket stitched to the inside of the cape. She slipped her statuette into it for safe keeping.

As she moved, the weight of beads sewn around the hem of the cape swung against her legs. It felt wonderful. Susan lifted her head and sailed through the door. *I feel like a princess.* She laughed to herself.

Susan and Teo were among the last to reach the pier. As they hurried down to the river, Susan paused to look. The sky was just getting light behind the desert hills, and in the smoky light of early dawn, Susan could see the Nile spread out at her feet. Mist rose from the water and drifted in the soft breeze blowing up the river. There was a smell of mud and the sleepy quack of ducks in the clicking reeds.

Flaming torches tied to posts on the floating pier lit the scene as people scurried about, carrying large boxes and chests. The reed pier lurched and jumped under her feet as she hurried along. The boat was large and grand and made of wood. It rose up high in the front and the back, and Susan saw a large steering board hanging over the stern. The steersman already stood there, watching the currents out in the river.

A little house stood high in the center of the boat. Not a house exactly. There was a roof, but the walls were curtains fluttering in the breeze.

Along both sides of the boat, Susan saw rowers sitting at their oars.

Harsheer awaited her. "Come on. Hurry up, girl. We want to get as far as possible in the cool of the day."

Susan jumped easily to the boat deck. Teo followed close behind, and the two of them moved immediately to the little house. Behind the curtains sleeping mats were laid out, and Susan sank thankfully onto the closest one.

She drifted back into sleep to the sound of the rowers' rhythm beaten on a small drum and the gurgle of water lapping on the side of the boat. They were on their way to Thebes.

CHAPTER 14

SUSAN'S POWER

Susan awoke to Harsheer shouting at the top of his voice.

"Hurry, hurry," he yelled over and over. The rowers' drum beat was much faster now.

Susan groaned and rolled onto her back as memory of all that had happened to her flooded back. Six months. Six months before she saw home again— if she saw home again. That was what worried her the most. She knew she could arrive at the time she left, but what if something happened and the crystal didn't grow? She would be stuck here thousands of years in the past, and her parents would never know what happened to her.

Her throat closed, and her eyes began to prickle. *Crying's no good*, she thought fiercely and clambered to her feet.

She was hot and sticky and thirsty and…Susan shook herself, straightened her sheath, and stuck her head in the air. *Remember, your name's Sinclair,* she thought and then giggled because actually her name, right now, was Princess Merit-Amen. Nobody at home would ever believe her. *Judy would have a fit.* Susan pushed aside the curtains and stepped out into the blazing sunlight.

The boat was flying over the water. The river surged on every side. They were in the middle of the stream where the water flowed the fastest. Susan smelled the sweat from the rowers.

"What's the big hurry?" she asked Harsheer, who sat on a cushion in the shade.

"We have to be in Thebes for the Opet festival, and the crystal must be started beforehand," he answered.

Harsheer held out a cup of water to her, so Susan sat down. She noticed the bottle containing the brew from last night nestled between Harsheer's legs.

Susan's head ached with questions.

"Why me?"

"Believe me"—Harsheer shook his head—"it wasn't my choice."

"So we're stuck with each other."

"If you ever want to get home, yes."

"What makes you think I'm the one you summoned?"

"Hmmmm." Harsheer stared off to the great cliffs in the distance. Susan thought he wasn't going to answer, but then he said, "It was the stone. You came with nothing—I deliberately summoned you with nothing. And the gods gave you a green stone the moment you arrived."

"It hurt my hand."

"There's always a price to pay in magic." Harsheer stared off to the horizon again.

They sat in silence. Susan sipped the water.

"And the feather, too." Harsheer went on as though there had been no pause. "The great hawk god Horus sent you a feather. You are protected by him. You are a great magician."

Susan sat quietly, sipping her water. *Let him think I'm powerful*, she thought. *I've got to get home.*

"You're a child. You don't know your potential. I'll teach you. We will make wondrous magics. Pharaoh will bow at our feet."

"I'm going home in six months," Susan retorted.

Harsheer looked disappointed and a little sad, but Susan didn't care. She stood up and stomped to the bow of the boat.

CHAPTER 15

INTO PHARAOH'S TOMB

"I need you properly dressed and ready to leave," Harsheer said as he popped the last of the grapes into his mouth.

Susan wiped her fingers on a napkin and picked up her drinking cup. "I thought you usually rested during the heat of the day," she said.

"Not today," Harsheer retorted. "Teo, have the princess ready. We inspect the royal tomb."

Teo bowed low and quickly drew Susan into the shelter.

Susan sat on a stool while Teo wove her sidelock and draped her in bracelets. Teo found her a pair of earrings that reached almost to Susan's shoulders, and she clasped skimpy sandals onto Susan's feet. Teo brought out a flask of perfumed oil and began to rub it into Susan's arms.

"Why all the preparation?" Susan asked.

"It's a great honor to visit the tomb of a pharaoh; you must be properly dressed, Princess."

"I didn't see any pyramid around here," Susan said, remembering the television show about Egyptian pyramids being tombs.

"That was many years ago, Princess. Now pharaohs are buried in great secret in hidden places—sacred places." Teo's eyes were big and round as she told Susan these things. "When the pharaoh leaves us to join the other gods, his earthly body is hidden away in a palace built for him for eternity."

Harsheer stuck his head through the curtains.

"Hurry up. We're landing," he said and rushed out again.

"I'll burn to a crisp out there in that sun," Susan said, looking out through the curtains. "Haven't you got a hat I could wear?"

"Princess." Teo looked shocked. "I am your shade carrier."

Teo slipped a cloak of the sheerest linen over Susan's shoulders. It fell in gentle folds all around her. "This will protect you from the sun," she said as she settled a wide beaded collar over it and stood back to admire her handiwork. "You look beautiful, Princess," she said, holding up a look-face.

Susan looked. *Weird*, she thought.

Susan stepped out into the blazing sun to see that the boat had been pulled to the shore.

Stepping to the side of the boat, Susan saw about three feet of muddy water between her and dry land. She looked at the dainty sandals on her feet and bent to take them off.

"Sssst." Harsheer grabbed her arm and pulled her upright. "Remember you're a princess."

Hori waded out from the shore. He was covered in mud up to his knees.

"Princess," he said and held out his arms.

Hori carried Susan across the mud and stood her carefully on dry ground.

Hori and another soldier carried Harsheer over, and then finally Hori carried Teo, very carefully, to dry land.

Susan walked over to stand beside Teo and immediately her sandals were scratchy with the sandy, dusty grit of the pathway. *I'm going to need Band-Aids if it's far to walk,* she thought, shaking her foot.

Two chairs were carried from the boat. Susan, sitting in a chair, was lifted and carried along by four soldiers. She gripped the arms tightly as the chair lurched up the steep path. Teo walked beside the chair, holding a large plume of feathers up to shade Susan's head.

The path led up a fairly stiff incline, and by the time the soldiers reached the top of the ridge, they were sweating and panting. Hori called a halt.

Susan hopped out of the chair gladly and walked around to stretch her legs. Teo slumped beside the water tank, but Harsheer paced back and forth, muttering to himself, anxiously looking at the sun's position and the pathway ahead.

Susan stared at the spectacular view laid out before her. She saw, stretched out, the entire expanse of the river. She saw trees growing in the water and decided that the river must be flooded way beyond its normal banks. Below her, the boat was tied to one of the last trees in the green strip that stretched along the riverbanks. Where Susan stood and in every direction except the river, the land was dry, dusty, and barren. The sunlight bounced off the light-colored rock and sand, making the air seem to dance.

On the far bank of the river, Susan saw a large city. The houses were low and mostly painted bright colors, but through the heat haze, she saw two huge structures at either end of the city. *They're probably temples*, she decided. Squinting against the glare, Susan thought she saw a roadway along the riverfront, joining the two temples.

"Drink this," Harsheer thrust a cup of water under her nose. "You've got to keep drinking out here."

"Thanks." Susan took the cup, and Harsheer immediately turned on his heel and marched back to where the soldiers rested.

While Susan sipped the water, Harsheer chivvied the soldiers to their feet.

She hurried to take her place on her chair again, glad she wasn't walking.

They traveled away from the river, into a dry, dusty valley where nothing grew. The sun glared off the soft yellow rock, so that Susan's eyes watered from the dazzle.

A guardhouse stood on the summit of the pass into the next valley. Two soldiers came running out and bowed low to Harsheer as their group hurried past.

The path broadened out just beyond the guardhouse, and Harsheer signaled a halt.

"Come on. Hurry up," Harsheer beckoned to Susan as she climbed stiffly from her chair. "Hurry, hurry."

Teo followed with the feather plume, but Harsheer waved her back.

"We go on alone," he said to Susan and marched resolutely into the valley.

Susan hurried after, stumbling on the gritty path in her dainty sandals.

They climbed over piles of broken rock and passed by an area where huge, elaborate doors sealed what looked like a tunnel into the rock cliff. Susan leaned against the door, panting heavily. Harsheer hurried on.

What a place. Susan drew in deep breaths until her heart stopped hammering. It was so quiet. The sun blazed off the rock, but it was shaded where Susan rested. She traced her fingers through the signs carved into the rock all around the door opening, but they meant nothing to her. *I wish I knew what it said,* she thought.

"That's the tomb of Tuthmosis I," Harsheer said. "His throne name was Aakheperkara. He was the first to be buried here." Harsheer grabbed her arm and hauled her along. "Come on," he said. "We must hurry."

Susan dug in her heels. "You, hurry, hurry. You don't say why, just expect me to follow along. I'm exhausted and hot."

"Stupid girl, we have to get the crystal growing in the tomb, and we have to get to Thebes tonight. Tomorrow is Opet." And as if that made it all sensible, he turned on his heel and marched off down the valley.

Susan followed.

Harsheer stopped at another door set into the valley wall. The excavations around the door looked newer, and Susan felt sharp edges when she ran her hand over the carvings.

Harsheer thrust a lit torch into her hands and pushed the door open. It creaked as it swung. Without hesitation Harsheer hurried along the corridor.

Susan held her burning torch high as she followed. After the burning desert outside, it was cold in the tomb. Her torch showed colorful pictures drawn on the walls. Susan shivered.

Harsheer ran down a flight of steps leading even farther into the depths. Susan felt the weight of stone above her head and stood looking around. Soon Harsheer's torchlight disappeared, and she was left in a small pool of light shed by her own torch. The dark seemed to reach for her. She thought she could hear small skitterings over the hiss of the burning torch. She hurried down the stairs after Harsheer.

There seemed only one direction to go, and she ran lightly down another corridor, not pausing to see what was drawn on the walls.

"Stop!" Harsheer's voice roared. The sound echoed and reechoed off the walls. Susan stood, stunned.

CHAPTER 16

GROW, CRYSTALS, GROW

"Stupid. Stupid." Harsheer pointed to the ceiling, and Susan saw a nest of spears aimed at the floor. He stood, shaking his head and muttering.

Carefully, Susan moved to the side of the corridor and began inching along the wall. She glanced once more at the spears and hugged the wall closer. She didn't dare breathe.

"It's to catch thieves," he said. "Keep up."

"Why?" Susan asked, sticking close to his heels.

"We can't have everyone just walking in down here, you know," Harsheer said airily.

"I nearly died back there." Susan gulped.

"Well, in the future, stick close. I would have been in trouble if you'd died before we started the crystals growing."

"Thanks for caring," Susan mumbled.

Eventually, after several more corridors and stairs, Harsheer and Susan entered a large chamber. Harsheer dipped his flaming torch into a brazier against the wall, and light flared up around them. The walls were painted with wonderful scenes of life. Susan could see people hunting, eating, dancing— everywhere she looked, the walls were covered with brightly painted pictures.

In the center of the room stood a massive stone carving. Susan traced the carvings with her fingers. "What's this?" she asked.

"That's the sarcophagus of the most royal pharaoh, Akheperenre."

"What's a sarcophagus?" Susan asked, and Harsheer mimicked her question as though he knew she would ask it.

"It's the encasing where the body of the pharaoh will lie for eternity," he said.

Susan shuddered. "Like a coffin?" She felt for the line around the side of the sarcophagus and could feel that the top half was a lid and would lift off. It was huge, and the lid fit perfectly. *My mother would love to see such a wonderful carving*, she thought sadly.

Harsheer moved to the back wall and began chipping at a small space. Soon he was banging away at the wall, mumbling and muttering to himself. First he chipped through the painting and then into the rock itself.

Susan walked around the sarcophagus to watch. Harsheer wasn't skilled at carving. He hit the chisel wrong, and blood sprang from his hand. He dropped everything and jumped around, sucking his hand like a small boy.

Susan picked up the chisel and hammer and moved to the hole.

"What's this for?" she asked.

"We need a niche for the crystals to grow in," Harsheer said around his hand.

"You hold my torch," Susan said and began chipping away at the stone. It was easy to cut, coming away in soft, flaky layers.

Susan expertly carved a deep niche. Harsheer pushed her aside and examined it closely.

"Yes, I knew I had the right magician," he said.

Huh. Susan shook her head.

With a flourish he produced the flask containing the liquid. In his other hand appeared a small pottery saucer with a disk rising in the center. He handed it to Susan.

"Position that in the niche," he ordered.

Susan felt bumps and ridges on the disk and put it close to the torch to see what was inscribed on the surface, but Harsheer stopped her.

"It's my secret," he said. "Just put it in the niche."

When it was positioned exactly as he wished, Harsheer moved forward with the alabaster flask.

"Say and do the same as me," he ordered and began gently pouring the liquid into the saucer.

Susan didn't understand the words he muttered, but she muttered them, too. As he poured, his other hand moved into patterns, and Susan made her hand move the same way.

"Om slessy," Harsheer said.

"Om slessy," Susan repeated.

The chanting went on as the liquid slowly slipped from the container into the saucer. Sometimes Harsheer shouted, and then Susan shouted, too.

Sometimes the words were sung, and Susan followed the notes as best she could.

In the back of her mind, whatever Susan said, and whatever her fingers did, her thoughts ran. *Please grow well, crystals. I need you, crystal. I miss you. Grow, crystal. Please, crystal.*

When all the fluid was in the saucer, the two of them sank to the floor to rest.

"Why here?" Susan asked.

"The tomb is finished and ready. The king is a young man still. Nothing will disturb it for the next six months. The crystals can grow here without any vibration to cause them to be small or flawed."

"How can you be sure it will be safe here?"

"I am the keeper of the royal tomb. Nobody can come in here without my permission. Nothing will disturb the crystals while they grow."

Susan wasn't so sure.

Before they left the tomb, Harsheer produced a piece of stiff cloth from somewhere and fastened it over the hole they had made. With mutterings and hand passes, he held it in place. The light of the torches suddenly went out, leaving the two of them in complete darkness.

Susan couldn't breathe. The weight of the rock and the darkness pressed in on her. She had never been anywhere as dark before.

Harsheer struck a spark and lit his torch again. With relief Susan held hers to the flame. When she checked the hole, she couldn't find it. The cloth had fused to the wall and taken on the pattern of the picture.

"That's amazing," she said, with her face close to the wall.

"Thank you," said Harsheer, leaning against the sarcophagus.

Susan ran her fingers lightly along the wall and could feel only a slight difference in the texture where the hole had been. Even knowing where it was she couldn't see the patch in the torchlight.

"Come on. Stop fussing." Harsheer hopped from foot to foot.

The two of them hurried out of the tomb.

The heat and glare hit Susan like a physical blow as Harsheer pushed the door open.

She leaned against the rock.

Harsheer gestured and produced sealing wax seemingly from the air.

"How do you do that?" Susan asked.

He looked at her sideways and smiled a secretive smile.

Quickly he sealed the doors and twisted a rope through the handles in a fancy pattern. He poured the wax onto the knot and pressed a large seal, which appeared in his hand, into the wax.

"No one may enter here. The crystals will grow, and in six months we will inspect the tomb again," Harsheer said, and he laughed.

That is not a nice laugh, Susan thought as she hurried after Harsheer.

CHAPTER 17
THEBES

Harsheer hurried everyone back to the boat. The only stop they made along the way was at the guardhouse. There, Harsheer informed the two guards that everything was in order in the tomb and that it was sealed.

"No one enters, on pain of death," he said sternly.

The guards nodded in solemn agreement.

Susan sank into her own thoughts. So much was happening so fast. The world she had entered was so rich and adventurous that she felt her own real life slipping away.

She stayed wrapped in her own thoughts throughout the evening meal and said nothing as the boat slipped into moorings on the river below the city. Harsheer seemed glad to have her quiet.

He hurried ashore as soon as the boat was tied up. He issued quick orders to Hori and then disappeared into the crowd on the road above the river. People stepped back to let him pass, Susan noticed.

It was deep evening by the time they left the boat. Their path took them through the temple grounds. The others hurried along but Susan stopped to stare. The group skirted the base of a needle of stone that speared into the sky. Susan brushed it with her hands. It was smooth and polished to the touch.

She had to lean way back to see the tops of the pillars supporting the roof that soared above her. They passed around a huge pool and through a gate in the wall, which led them into the palace.

The arrangement of rooms was totally confusing to Susan. She followed Hori and Teo through endless corridors and across several gardens and courtyards. Finally they entered a set of rooms.

"This is your suite, Princess." Hori waved his arm to indicate that they should enter.

Susan flopped onto the bed and fell asleep before Teo could pull the beads from her sidelock.

CHAPTER 18

DAY ONE

Susan woke to a low droning sound. It went on and on, so low that she had to listen hard to be sure it was a sound. A muffled drum beat added to the drone, and then higher voices broke in on top, and Susan realized she was listening to people singing.

It's like the morning song they sang on the river, she thought, rolling over onto her back. In the light seeping in through the blinds on the open spaces at the top of the wall, Susan could see Teo sleeping soundly on her pallet in the corner.

It was a nice room; the walls were colored soft blue and one wall was painted with a river scene. There were rushes and palm trees standing in the water. It looked cool and shady. In the depths Susan noticed a little reed boat. It was empty and pulled into the bank as though the paddlers had gone for a walk. She lay there, staring dreamily at the picture, comfortable under her light linen sheet.

Thump, thump, thump. Someone banged on her door. Not knocking—banging.

Teo, leaped up with a squeal. "I'm awake," she wailed. "Oh my, oh my. We're late." She crumpled to the floor, sobbing piteously.

Sighing, Susan threw back her covers and searched around for her sheath.

Thump, thump, thump.

The singing came closer.

Bang.

The door flew open, catching Susan and flinging her into the wall with Teo. She rose angrily. "What are you doing?" she shouted. "I am Merit-Amen, daughter of the Magician Harsheer."

Standing in the doorway was a large man with a worried look on his face. He was grandly dressed. His white kilt was tied with a fancy beaded belt that folded down the front of his kilt. His chest was covered with a collar of intricately patterned beads. In his hands he carried a large sheet of paper, and he was consulting it.

"I'm Senmut, and you're late, that's what you are," he barked. "You're holding up the procession."

Susan looked past his shoulder and saw the passageway filled with grandly dressed people all craning to see into her room. A few were laughing behind their hands.

She reached over and slammed the door in his face. "Quick, quick." She rushed to Teo. "What's happening?"

Teo bawled louder. "I'll be sent to the fields," she wailed.

"Stop that this instant," Susan insisted. "Tell me what's going on."

"It's Opet." Teo gulped and rushed to the chest by the bed. "I should have you dressed for the procession." She shook out a fresh sheath for Susan. It was white and of very fine material.

The thumping on the door began again.

Susan grabbed the sheath and quickly threw it over her head.

Teo, still sniffling, drew a beaded collar around Susan's shoulders. It was smaller than the one she usually wore. She raised her eyebrows to Teo in question.

"That's the one the magician said you should wear this morning," she said, flicking her fingers.

The door flew open again. "What is the meaning of this delay?" demanded an imperious voice.

Susan whirled, angry. Then stood, mouth open, staring. In her doorway stood the most magnificent woman she had ever seen. Standing tall and straight, the woman wore a sheath similar to her own, but every inch of her exposed skin was dusted in gold. The woman glittered in the morning light streaming through the gap in the wall. Her head was covered in an elaborate wig of curls and ringlets. Precious stones gleamed in the coils. Her face showed that she was used to command as she imperiously stared down at Susan.

"Princess Merit-Amen, you are late. And we are waiting. Join the procession *now*."

Susan jumped and hurried toward the door, to obey.

"Now, now, Hatti," another voice interrupted. "She can't go out in the sun like that. Look how pale her skin is."

A man as magnificently dressed as the woman came up beside her. Susan saw that he looked as relaxed as the woman looked tense. He had a smile on his face and a twinkle in his eye when he looked at her.

"Princess Merit-Amen," he said and bowed to her. "I am Akheperenre, and you are holding up my procession. We have to escort the god Amun, He Who Is Silent, to visit with his wife and son, and if we don't get started soon, we'll be doing it in the full heat of the day. Please hurry." And, so saying, he shut the door again.

The pharaoh. Susan stood, dumbfounded. Teo quickly rubbed oil into her head and arms, smeared a dark powder under her eyes, like eye shadow in reverse. She added bangles and rings and declared Susan ready.

"Where's my shoes?"

"No shoes, Princess." Teo shook her head and moved to open the door.

"Wait, wait, what am I supposed to do?"

Teo thought for a minute. "I don't know, Princess. I don't know." She flicked her hands helplessly.

Susan braced herself and took a big breath. "OK, let's go."

"Not me, Princess, just you." Teo opened the door before Susan could protest.

They were still waiting. The singing became louder as the door opened. Susan ducked her head but saw the queen scowl at her disapprovingly.

"That's better," said Akheperenre. "Why don't you stand in there with Neferure and Useramen, and they can look after you?"

Susan shuffled into the line. She smiled shyly at the two. The girl, Neferure, gave her a haughty glare. The boy, Useramen, looked like he could hardly contain his laughter.

The procession wound on through the palace. They stopped at other doors, and when Senmut knocked, the people came out quickly, bowing low to the king and queen.

Susan shuffled along with the others, and she watched everything closely. *I have to learn very quickly, or I'll be executed or something*, she thought.

CHAPTER 19

OPET

Eventually the procession from the palace wove its way out into a courtyard. A group of priests stood in their robes, singing and chanting. The voices rose and fell over the constant sound of a deep, low drum. With everyone assembled the whole parade moved off across the courtyard. Positioned as she was, close behind the pharaoh and queen, Susan had a wonderful view of everything as events unfolded.

As their party wound through the temple grounds, they were joined by another group of priests. These carried an elaborate boat on their shoulders. The boat was painted red and covered in gold, which glinted in the sun. The little house in the center of the boat had richly decorated curtains that were tied tightly shut. Harsheer, carrying a long staff of gold, led that group of priests. The pharaoh and queen fell into place behind the boat, and they all paraded out through the huge doors in the wall of the temple grounds. Susan saw the River Nile spread before them.

Susan leaned over toward Neferure. "Who is in the fancy boat?"

The princess looked to neither right nor left. Her expression didn't change.

Susan felt a touch on her arm. "It's the god Amun who is in the boat, new Princess," whispered Useramen.

As they moved beyond the wall, Susan saw there were hundreds of people lining the riverbank. Children played around the feet of the adults, running and chasing one another in excitement. The crowd made an awed murmuring sound that soughed over the steady beat of the drum and the chanting of the priests.

The procession moved to the edge of the river, and the priests waded in and carefully placed Amun's boat on a floating platform that looked to have been built especially to carry Amun along the river.

A windy sigh escaped from the crowd. They began to chant with the priests.

As the priests waded back to the riverbank, they carried ropes that unfurled from the platform. The first rope went to Pharaoh and the queen, who took it up. The next was handed to Neferure and Useramen. They grasped it tight, and Susan reached to grasp it, too, but Neferure jerked it out of her hands with a hiss.

Susan felt like hundreds of eyes all up and down the riverbank were boring into her. What could she do now? She stood, uncertain.

Useramen took her hands and put them onto the rope next to his. "Here, Merit-Amen, we all have to pull. It's a great privilege to pull the god down the river to join with his wife and son."

Susan grasped the rope gratefully. It felt like a lifeline. She watched carefully to see what everyone else did.

Over the hubbub of the crowd and the chanting, a gong sounded. It struck a deeper note than the drum. Susan felt the tone vibrating in her chest. Everyone began to pull on the ropes. At first the platform just bobbed on the rippled water, but gradually it began to inch along the shore.

Susan pulled with the rest. She felt exhilarated to be part of such a large crowd all doing the same thing for the same reason. The people watched and cheered at each pull. The procession pulled with a will, and the little boat on its platform gathered speed. The road felt smooth and even under her feet, and Susan had no trouble keeping up.

The boat was moving merrily along when they came to a dip in the road where the way led right down to the water's edge. The road became muddy. Susan felt the ooze between her toes at each step.

At the lowest point in the dip, about six inches of water lay across the path. The mud was slick and black. Susan was never sure how Neferure did it, but somehow she snagged Susan's feet and pushed on her arm at the same time, and Susan went down in the slick. Useramen skidded but managed to keep his feet, jerking the rope from her hands. The crowd roared laughing. Susan scrambled up, slick, black, and uncomfortable. She grabbed the rope and continued on. What else could she do?

From then on, Susan heard the wave of laughter as she passed. No one else fell. She was the only muddy one.

The day turned gray for her, and she plodded mechanically along. *Six months. Six months of this awful place. How will I do it?*

Finally, the procession and the boat on the river reached the temple at the north end of the city. The priests waded in and bore the boat into the temple on their shoulders.

CHAPTER 20

A FRIEND

The procession broke up with much shaking of shoulders and laughter. The paraders wandered off into town. There were chairs waiting for the pharaoh and queen, who sat and were carried away on sturdy shoulders.

Susan stood, uncertain what to do. No one cared about her. Harsheer was busy in the temple, settling the god in with his wife and son. Teo was back in the palace—probably crying. Susan looked around and couldn't see one friendly face.

Well, at least I can find my way back to the palace, she thought and turned back along the road.

The sun was hot and beat down on her exposed head. The beads across her chest itched as she became sweaty. The mud that had dried in the sun became wet again as sweat trickled down her skin.

"Ah, the mud princess." Someone spoke lightly behind her. She whirled around to find Prince Useramen smiling at her.

His black youth lock was plaited with little silver beads, and his laughing brown eyes were lined with dark eye shadow, the same as Teo had smeared under hers. *Like footballers when they play night games under lights*, Susan saw. He stood about the same height as her and his kilt was clean.

"Can't you say something nice instead of teasing me?" It sounded lame even to her. Susan shook her head.

The prince laughed again. "Why wouldn't I comment on the mud? You must like it, or you wouldn't still be covered in it." His eyes strayed to the river.

Stupid, stupid Susan. She followed his glance and noticed small children and adults all along the banks, bathing in the waters of the Nile. Susan let out a whoop and ran down the bank and straight into the cool, swift river. She executed a shallow dive and swam through a tangle of legs underwater. She felt the clinging mud slip from her body.

As she broke the surface, she heard another splash behind her, but the water felt so good slipping over her body that she set out stroking against the current. Even with the weight of the beaded collar around her neck and the bangles on her arms, she felt free and cool. She swam for quite a distance. When she finally tired, she turned back toward the bank and pulled herself onto a floating pier jutting into the river.

Susan felt the sun drawing the water from her skin. *There's no need for a towel here,* she thought. She rolled onto her stomach and stared lazily out across the river. From her position, she could see across the shallows to the broader river beyond. In the distance were the sun-bleached cliffs she had climbed with Harsheer the day before.

Only yesterday they had started the crystals growing in the pharaoh's tomb. *Grow well, my crystal.* She sent her thoughts out across the water. *Grow well.*

Susan finally noticed the sounds of steady splashing coming closer. Peering over the edge of the pier, she saw the prince paddling toward her. He seemed to be hurrying, but he swam with a kind of dog paddle. He moved slowly through the water. The pier heaved and bobbed as he pulled himself out of the river beside her.

"Now that the mud is gone, what will I call you?" he asked.

"My name is Su…Merit-Amen," she said and held out her hand.

The prince ignored her hand but bowed his head. "Welcome to our land, Merit-Amen. We hear in the palace that you are from very far away."

Susan felt the centuries like a chasm at his words and nodded in agreement.

"Some in the palace believe that you are from Harsheer's estates and come not from another land at all." Prince Useramen lifted his eyebrows in question.

"Oh, no, I'm from far away. I'm not sure how I can convince you of that." Susan wasn't sure why she cared whether the prince believed her, except that he was the first person to show her any kindness since she arrived.

"Oh, I believe," said Useramen. "No one around here can swim like you. So swift, so easy, you cut through the water faster than any of us, even though we've been in the river since we could crawl."

"It's easy. We all swim that way where I come from. It's called the Australian crawl."

"And you are from this…Aus…Aus… place?"

"Oh no, everyone in the world swims that way now, even in the Olympics."

"Ah, Aus…that place is in Greece?"

My world is as strange to him as this one is to me, Susan realized. "I'll teach you to swim that way if you like," she said to change the subject.

"Thank you, Merit-Amen. I would like that." The prince bowed his head. "And I will teach you how to live in the palace. Your customs are very different, I think."

He doesn't know the half of it.

They spent the next hour or so splashing around in the water off the dock. They left their beads and bangles in a heap on the pier. Useramen learned quickly. It was easy to get his feet kicking correctly, and his arms moved OK, but it was coordinating the breathing that was the trick. They splashed and spluttered in the shallows until he felt confident, and then they struck out toward the river proper. They turned where the current became strong and raced each other back to the pier. They pulled themselves out of the water, laughing and happy.

"Useramen, that was the most fun I've had since I've been in your land," Susan said, wringing the water from her youth lock.

"Call me Djus. My friends do," he said.

"Call me Susan. That's my name in my land."

"Susan." Djus's eyes lit up. "Susan, really?" He jumped to his feet and ran pattering along the ramp to the shore. There he picked a lily growing on the water's edge and brought it back to her.

"Susan," he said. "Lily."

Susan took the waxy white flower into her hands and softly stroked the petals. "Really?" she murmured.

They prepared to return to the palace, and Djus slipped easily into the beads and necklets he had been wearing. Susan struggled to get hers untangled. Djus came over to help her with it, and fastening it at the back of her neck, he started to laugh again.

"I'm sorry, but you looked so funny this morning. And that incompetent little hitite wailing and bawling...." Djus broke off into laughter.

Now with a friend to share the morning's adventure, it didn't seem so bad to Susan, either, and she laughed with him.

"Why does Teo cry all the time?" she asked.

"Oh, that's because she's far from home and a captive, and some of them just go like that. I suppose she misses her home. You'd think they'd be happy to be living in the wonders of Egypt, but some never get over it and cry and sob forever. It can be very annoying."

"You mean she was captured in a war or something?"

"Yes, probably. Pharaoh's generals brought back hundreds of captives from his last war with the Hyksos. She definitely comes from north of us. Akheperenre gave most of them away to his people. She probably went to Harsheer as a reward for some service."

Susan was going to speak and then decided to keep her mouth firmly closed. *After all in our times people get uprooted by wars, too, and end up in refugee camps and things*, she thought.

Once her jewelry was settled to Djus's satisfaction, they climbed back up to the road and walked along in the crowd toward the palace. They were friends now, and it made everything she looked at seem different to Susan. The crowds seemed friendly, the Nile looked beautiful, and the cooking smells coming from some of the houses made her mouth water.

They walked in companionable silence until they arrived at the palace.

"I'll see you at the feast tonight, Susan," Djus said and turned to take his leave. But Susan, looking around in bewilderment, asked him to stay.

"I've no idea where my room is," she confessed shyly. "Can you show me, please?"

"Of course, but you should train that girl of yours better. She should be here waiting for you with cool, perfumed towels."

Djus bowed to her at her own door, turned, and hurried down the corridor.

Susan entered the room, hoping there would be something to eat before she had her afternoon nap.

CHAPTER 21
THE FEAST

Teo told Susan that the feast on the first night of Opet was the most exciting and lavish feast of the year.

Preparing took ages. It was fun to dig into the chests and boxes Harsheer had provided. There were so many wonderful garments. All light and skimpy and white. *Easier to wash, I guess.* But the jewelry!

The jewelry was lavish and heavy. Chests and boxes fell open to reveal bracelets, necklets, anklets, hairclips, even rings. Every color. Every texture. There were lots of shiny stones and spangles, too. Tiny colored beads woven into intricate patterns formed collars that clipped around her neck and reached out to her shoulders and down onto her chest. As Susan moved, she sparkled in the sunlight.

Teo plucked out all her eyebrows and then drew sweeping lines in their place. She dusted Susan's face and arms with a powder that sparkled in the light

The sheath she wore was pleated in intricate folds. Silver and gold threads woven into the light, airy fabric made the skirt glitter in the sunlight when Susan twirled around. Her youth lock was tightly braided and gleaming with beads and shiny balls. Silver bells woven into the end tinkled when she tossed her head.

Her sandals and bracelets held matching bells so that Susan loved the sound of her movement. *If Judy could see me now.* The fleeting thought skipped through her mind, but she pushed it down. Now was not the time to be pining for home. She had six months to live in this world, and she decided to make the most of it. *It's not every day you get to be a princess.*

And by the time Susan stood ready, she looked and felt like a princess.

Susan held her head high and stepped around the room.

"It's time for you to leave, Princess," Teo said with a bow.

Susan's stomach gave a lurch. "But where do I go, and what do I do?"

Teo shook her head. "I don't know. I was told to have you ready. You're the princess. Don't you know?" And she shrugged and turned away to tidy up.

Susan eyed the corner of the room. It would be so easy to just sink down and shut her eyes. *Come on,* she told herself. *This is an adventure. You're a princess. Smarten up.*

She squared her shoulders. "Teo," she said. "I want you to learn this palace from top to bottom. I'm sick of being in the dark and not knowing where to go."

Teo squealed and started to cry again. "I've never been here before, Merit-Amen. Please. I just want to stay here."

"No, you'll go out and learn about the palace and what goes on here," Susan said determinedly. "I need to know, and you are going to have to help me. And if you don't, I'll...I'll...send you to the fields."

Teo drew a huge, shuddering breath. "I'll go, Princess. I'll learn," she whispered.

"Good, then I'm off to find my own way." Susan left immediately—before her courage could fail her.

Once she stepped into the corridor, Susan had no problem figuring out where the feast was. She could hear it. Raucous laughter and music swelled in the air. She followed the sounds.

Susan peered nervously around the opening into the feasting area. By the noise it seemed there were hundreds of people present.

The celebration occupied one of the inner courts of the palace. Susan saw musicians playing at one end of the courtyard. She didn't recognize any of the instruments they played, but she quite liked the music. All the people at the feast lay around on the floor on cushions. The little tables beside them held small dishes with food.

The people sparkled in the lamplight. Everyone seemed to be wearing their best clothes and the smells that wafted toward Susan were overpowering—a mingling of flowers and spicy food.

A door attendant hurried over to Susan and, bowing low, thrust a flower into her hands. "A flower for a flower," he said.

It was blue and had many petals. *I've seen these floating in the river,* Susan remembered. The attendant held out a woven basket to her, and Susan saw that it contained small colored cones. Susan hesitated, not sure what they were, and the attendant selected one of the cones and held it out to her. Susan accepted it hesitantly; it felt waxy in her fingers and smelled of the same perfume as her flower. She peered around the door to see if she could see what she was supposed to do with it.

Sighing, the attendant took it back from her. "Allow me, Princess," he offered.

Susan nodded, and the attendant dropped a little hot wax from a candle onto the top of her head and stuck the little cone to her scalp. *Oh, right,* Susan thought, *now I walk into the room with this stuck to my head, and everyone laughs, and I die right there.*

"*Princess Merit-Amen,*" the attendant announced in a huge voice. There was a sudden hush in the room, and a rustling as people turned toward the door.

"I've decided to eat in my room," Susan said and turned away quickly, but Harsheer rushed up and grabbed her arm.

"At last you're here. You're late." He looked her over quickly. "Well, at least you look civilized now. No more mud, I hope. Now stop dawdling. I have to present you to Akheperenre and Hatshepsut."

Susan hung back. "But what will I say to them?"

Harsheer shrugged. "You don't need to say anything. Just bow and smile, and you'll be fine. Now hurry up, girl." Harsheer dragged her into the courtyard.

Susan tried to keep pace with Harsheer, but it was all so strange. Her eyes darted everywhere at once. She noticed with relief that everyone was wearing the little cones on their heads. The pharaoh and his queen were seated in chairs at one end of the courtyard, and Harsheer towed her through the cushions and tables toward them. They were halfway across the courtyard when a gong sounded and a group of serving girls came quickly into the room, carrying more bowls of food on trays. They wore beaded belts around their waists, and that was all. Susan looked once; she looked twice. All the serving girls were naked. Surprised, Susan stopped in her tracks.

"Come on." Harsheer yanked on her arm. Susan tried to keep her balance, but her foot caught on one of the cushions, and she tripped. She almost hit a little table, but managed to keep her feet; she stumbled a couple of steps and then stepped right in the middle of a very soft cushion. Down she went, sprawling among a group of feasters. One of them careened into a table, which collapsed with a crash, sending bowls flying. The impact of her fall caused the little cone on her head to fly off. It whizzed across the room and fell with a splash into a bowl on Princess Neferure's table.

The princess leaped to her feet, screaming and making a terrible fuss. Susan rose slowly to her feet and in embarrassment began to help the others at the table sit upright. Harsheer glared at her.

"I'm sorry," she mumbled.

Harsheer snorted deep in his throat, turned on his heel, and stalked across the courtyard, leaving Susan standing. Serving girls came running forward with cloths to help the guests who had been splattered with food from the smashed bowls. Gradually Neferure quieted down, and Susan got herself upright. She smoothed her sheath and tried to recapture the feeling of being a princess, but it was useless, and she turned quietly toward the door.

Susan had stepped no more than three paces when she heard a quiet voice behind her. "Princess Merit-Amen, I have saved a place for you at my table." Susan turned, and there was Djus, bowing before her. He stepped close and, taking her hand, whispered in her ear, "Never let them see you're upset, Susan. Keep your head up and show them you don't care. They'll all be tripping over the cushions by the end of the night and thinking it great fun."

Susan squeezed his hand gratefully and straightened her back. She stuck her head in the air and followed where Djus led. She concentrated more on how she moved than where she went, and so she found herself standing before the king and queen.

Djus bowed.

Susan bowed.

Queen Hatshepsut, magnificently dressed, sat rigidly on her chair. She stared down at Susan haughtily. "I suppose it will be left to me to teach you court manners, girl. You are much too wild for us here. If I don't do it, no one will, as usual."

Susan hung her head.

At pressure on her hand from Djus, she looked up and saw the pharaoh smiling at her. "My dear, you're a breath of fresh air. These parties are usually so dull in the first hours, and you've given me more entertainment than the dancers." He waved his hands. "And you only cost me a table and a few bowls, whereas the dancers cost me a field of wheat." An attendant filled the wine bowl the pharaoh waved at him. He drank deeply and then continued. "I think I want to kiss your cheek."

Djus released her hand, and Susan rose on tip-toes, putting her cheek up to the pharaoh. He bent slowly and gave her a kiss, and Susan heard him whisper to her, "Be careful of Neferure. You have an enemy there."

Susan straightened in surprise and bowed low. The pharaoh had his nose in his drinking cup and said no more.

Susan and Djus wove through the cushions until they reached a table where two of his friends awaited them.

Their names were Nebka and Dauuf, and they were lolling on the cushions, looking relaxed and comfortable. They looked friendly enough, and Susan sank thankfully onto the cushions.

"Here, try some of this," Nebka suggested, holding out a small bowl to her.

Susan didn't feel particularly hungry, but the spicy smell made her mouth water, and so she reached for the bowl.

"Try not to splash it on yourself," Nebka said.

Susan looked up quickly, embarrassed all over again, but she saw his smile and his eyes danced with humor.

"Shut up, Nebka," Djus said. "Here, use the bread to soak it up. It's very good. Don't take any notice of Nebka. He teases everyone."

Susan sighed. Djus to the rescue again. The food tasted lightly spiced and succulent. She tried a little from each of the bowls the boys passed to her.

Nebka, Susan noticed, had big ears that kind of stuck out. He had laughing eyes and very thick eyebrows. He was chubby, with a round face. He had a long scar running along the side of his right arm. He often rubbed at it as they talked.

When Dauuf stood, Susan saw that he was tall and slim. His beaded collar hung crookedly around his neck. His nose had a distinctive hook to it. He never seemed to be still. There was always some part of him that was moving, tapping time to the music, reaching for a new plate, patting at Nebka's or Djus's arms.

Dauuf left the table and wove skillfully through the cushions, and when he returned, he was holding a new cone for Susan in his hand. "Here, I got you a new one," he said. "I thought you would rather that than try to retrieve your other one from Neferure."

The boys laughed, and after a moment's hesitation, Susan joined in. She felt so clumsy here.

Then she thought how funny she must have looked sprawling among the guests, and it got funnier and funnier.

"Ah, Mud Princess, you are a welcome addition to our group." Nebka chuckled with tears running from his eyes. "You are going to be a source of much mischief—I can tell."

"That may be," said Dauuf, leaning forward, "but Neferure doesn't look too happy about it."

Susan peered across the courtyard from under her lashes, and sure enough, Neferure was glaring at them. Susan ducked her head.

"Who is she?" she asked Djus.

"Neferure is the daughter of the One and Hatshepsut," Djus replied quite formally.

"Why doesn't she like me?"

"Why does the Nile flow?" was all the answer Djus gave. He shrugged and looked a little embarrassed.

"Neferure is Neferure," Dauuf chipped in as though that explained everything.

Djus shook himself and turned to her, smiling. "At the end of Opet, we are all going boating on the river. Would you like to come with us?"

"Yes, I would," Susan said, glad to have found some friends. "I'm not sure what Harsheer will say about it, though."

"Harsheer will be busy," Djus said with certainty.

"All right then, I'd love to come."

It was quickly arranged, and Djus, without asking, arranged to come get her from her rooms.

As the evening wore on, the guests became louder and louder. Susan noticed that the serving girls were still serving lavish cups of wine and beer to the tables, and most of the guests seemed merrily drunk. Susan felt more relaxed, too, and sank back into the cushions, letting the boy's conversation wash over her. Nebka and Dauuf did most of the talking. Djus seemed to listen mostly, although when he did speak, the others listened.

They were a lighthearted group, who seemed comfortable in one another's company. *I'm lucky to have met Djus today*, Susan thought contentedly.

"Susan, Susan." Djus was whispering close to her ear and shaking her shoulder.

Susan woke with a start. "What's happening? Where…" Everything came rushing back, and Susan knew exactly where she was.

"You need to leave," Djus said, smiling.

"You're right." Susan smiled. "Thanks."

The three stood up with her. Susan was ready to walk straight to the door, but Djus took her arm, and they went in a more leisurely fashion. They stopped at several tables along the way, chatting with people, smiling, nodding. Nebka usually warned people to watch out and move any bowls that might be on the table, and people laughed, and Susan laughed, too. Gradually they moved toward the door. Susan's head was a blur.

She didn't know who she had met or if she would even recognize anyone again. Most seemed a little drunk anyway.

Finally they reached the doorway into the courtyard. Nebka and Dauuf melted into the dark, and Djus escorted her back to her rooms.

"I don't want you wandering the courtyards all night," he said with a smile.

Susan slumped against the door and smiled, too. "Thank you," was all she could say. She opened the door to find the room in darkness.

"Really," Djus said sharply, "where is your maid? Where's the light? She is very incompetent. It's too bad that you should be treated like this."

A squeal came from the darkness, followed by a sob.

"It's OK, Djus. She's here," Susan whispered. A faint glow shone in the room where Teo lit a lamp. "Good night," Susan said and shut the door.

Teo rushed forward to help her out of her jewelry. Tears rolled down her face, and she sniffed pitiably.

"Oh, stop that, Teo," Susan snapped. "Honestly, you need to dry up."

Susan fell instantly asleep as soon as the linen sheet drifted over her.

CHAPTER 22
SOLITUDE

The Opet festival lasted for fourteen days. Every day the palace rang with the sounds of music and laughter. People slept in corridors and drank far too much beer and wine. The celebrations and noise went on and on.

Every night of Opet, Susan shared a dining table with Djus, Dauuf, and Nebka. It made it easier to walk into the courtyard, knowing she had friends there. Neferure glared at her from across the room, but Susan got used to the princess's icy stares. Harsheer ignored her, and that suited Susan fine. She stayed out of his way as much as she could.

I don't want him thinking up some new magic to work with me, she thought.

Susan used the time to explore the palace grounds. Nobody took much notice of her and Teo as they walked through the courtyards and passages. One afternoon, they happened upon a beautiful garden. Trees and flowers surrounded a large pond on which water lilies floated. Two beautiful ibis stood in the shallows, intently eyeing the pond depths. Quiet surrounded the garden, and Susan sank thankfully onto a stone bench in the shade of the tree.

What would happen in her life next? As Susan thought back over her life since Mrs. Coleman had given her the crystal, it all seemed a jumble to her. She supposed she would get used to constantly being among strangers and in strange places, but in the quiet, Susan had to admit to herself that she missed her home. *I wonder what Mum and Dad are doing right now,* she thought wistfully.

CHAPTER 23

PICNIC

"Prince Useramen told me to tell you that we are going boating in the reeds today."

"Yes, Princess," Teo mumbled as she combed out Susan's youth lock.

Teo looks as happy as usual, Susan thought, sitting still for the pulling and waiting for the inevitable sniffing.

"Are you getting to know your way around the palace?" Susan asked.

"Yes, Princess," Teo muttered, rubbing oil into Susan's arms. She had perfumed it with lotus blossom, and the sweet smell drifted in the cooler morning air. The sun blazed through the wall slit, so Susan knew it would be scorching later in the day.

"Hori helped me," Teo offered, and Susan noticed her face soften and a small light of happiness show through.

Ah, thought Susan. "I'd better take a hat," she said.

"Oh, no, Egyptian people don't wear hats. I will go with you and cover you with a shade—that's my job." Teo moved to lift the feather fan from the corner of the room where it rested against the wall.

"I don't think it's that sort of trip, Teo. Why don't you ask Hori to show you around the palace some more? I really need you to be able to find everything."

Teo smiled. Her face lit up. It was the first smile Susan had seen.

Teo is really quite pretty. At least I won't have to listen to her sobbing all day.

Djus, Nebka, and Dauuf arrived, laughing and shouting.

Susan was ready to leave, but Djus stopped her at the door.

"Where is your princess's drying cloth and spare sheath and oil for after bathing?" he barked at Teo.

Teo squealed and dissolved into tears.

"Enough of that," Djus snapped. "Hurry, girl. We don't want to wait."

Teo quickly assembled the requested items and thrust them into a drawstring bag.

Susan took it and quickly left the room with the boys. The day could only get better.

They hurried down to the pier, but the others beat them to it. Neferure was there with several other boys and two girls that Susan didn't know.

"Who said you could come?" One of the girls stuck her face rudely in Susan's.

Djus stepped in front of her. "I invited the princess Merit-Amen to join us, Peri," he said and guided Susan down to his little reed boat.

The others all settled into boats as well. Nebka and Dauuf hopped into the one next to Djus and Susan. By the time they were settled, Nebka had splashed them thoroughly with his paddle, and Dauuf had leaned over to help Susan stow her bag in the back of the boat and managed to overturn himself and Nebka into the water.

Susan gripped the sides until her knuckles showed white as their boat dipped and swung wildly in the backwash from Nebka's and Dauuf's antics. Susan felt the reed bundles give under her hands.

Djus leaned close in the confusion. "Have you ever paddled a boat before?"

Susan shook her head. "I've seen them paddle on television."

"Well, here's your paddle. Try not to make us look too silly." Djus laughed. He pushed off from the floating pier, and Susan felt the boat flex and give around her. She clung to the paddle as though it could save her.

"Dip it in the water once or twice, Mud Princess," Nebka called as they paddled by.

So Susan did and found it wasn't difficult. She just dipped as hard as she could and let Djus do all the steering and whatever other refinements there were to managing the little boat. They soon drew level with Nebka and Dauuf, and the two boats skimmed over the water, going faster and faster. They pulled way ahead of the other three boats and were soon deep among the reeds.

Susan enjoyed the pull in her shoulder muscles and the feeling that she and Djus were together and friends. Nebka and Dauuf were fun, too.

The boats finally drove into the shore, and Djus and Dauuf jumped quickly out and rushed toward a large rock standing in the mud. Djus tripped Dauuf, and the two rolled over and over, always scrambling toward the rock.

"They always do that," said Nebka, climbing out of his boat and pulling it farther onto the shore.

Susan followed his example, and when the two boats were on the shore side by side, she asked him, "Should we run for the rock, too?"

Dauuf shrugged. "Nah, let them do it. I'm too hot."

The two flopped down with their feet in the water. Shortly Djus and Dauuf joined them and splashed into the river to get clean. The other three boats arrived, and soon everyone was lying in the shallows, keeping cool. Susan stayed as far away from Neferure as she could.

Susan lay in the cool water, thinking of recent events. Djus, Nebka, and Dauuf joked and laughed around her and yelled back and forth to the other groups as well. She felt as though she belonged at last, and it was becoming more and more interesting. Now that she had some friends here, she saw that the six-month waiting period might not be too bad. After all, how often did anyone get to be a princess? Deep in her thoughts and feelings of peace, Susan idly swatted at a mosquito that buzzed around her head. Then there were two mosquitoes buzzing. She looked down and saw that there were about twenty of them on her stomach and feeding on her. She slapped at them in annoyance.

There's always something, she thought in disgust, slapping madly. As many as she killed, more landed.

Djus sat up. "What's happening?" He saw the mosquitoes all over Susan and began brushing the ones off her back. "You're covered in bites," he said. Djus sniffed at his fingers where there was a slight trace of the oil Teo had rubbed into Susan's skin that morning. "Lotus," he said.

"I like lotus," Susan said, brushing at her legs.

"So do I. So do mosquitoes," Djus replied.

Susan couldn't argue with him there. Her body was covered with red spots—and they itched.

Djus pushed her into the water.

Susan came up gasping for breath and prepared to strike out for a swim, but Djus was right beside her.

"Don't swim," he said. Susan stood in the water up to her neck instead. "The mosquitoes can't get you here," Djus explained. "Whatever possessed that stupid girl of yours to put lotus oil on your skin when you were spending the day on the river?"

Susan shrugged, feeling miserable. "She didn't know, I guess."

Djus handed her a dollop of mud and, taking another handful, began to scrub the oil off her back.

Between the two of them, they soon had all the oil off; the water around them stirred black and cloudy with mud. While they scrubbed, Djus explained that when spending the day outdoors on the riverbank, it was necessary to use heavier oil and that there were special blends of plants and roots that kept the mosquitoes at bay.

"I have oil with me, Susan, and we will put that on instead. It will protect you."

They turned to wade from the water and found all the others lined along the bank, watching them.

"The mud princess in her element." Peri laughed.

Susan hesitated and ducked down into the water again, but Djus forced her out onto the bank in front of him.

"Oh no, Peri, not the mud princess anymore, but the melon princess." Neferure laughed, holding up a melon she was eating so all could see the spotty skin.

Susan's eyes flashed at her, and for a moment, she noticed just a flicker of uncertainty in Neferure's cold and arrogant eyes.

I won't let her worry me, Susan decided and walked haughtily out of the water.

Dauuf helped pull her the last few steps. "Here, Merit-Amen, use my oil. It's a good blend for the day."

Susan accepted the oil gratefully and lathered it on liberally. *It's like a cross between suntan oil and insect repellent,* she thought to herself.

Several of the party kicked a ball around, and others had gone into the water to swim. Djus came and sat beside her. "I have a plan," he said. Dauuf and Nebka crowded in close to listen.

They all nodded.

Djus sauntered over to where Neferure sat with her friends. "Let's have a swimming race," he offered.

Neferure turned from her friends, and her eyes narrowed. "Why? You know I can always beat you in the water."

Djus ran his foot through the sand. "Well, yes, but Merit-Amen tells me she's a very good swimmer and that where she comes from everyone swims, but there is no Nile, so I don't know how she can."

"This sounds like one of your tricks," Peri sneered, shaking her head.

"Still"—Neferure looked over to where Susan sat itching her leg—"I'd like to see her beaten. She doesn't belong with us."

It was soon arranged. Susan and Djus would swim against Neferure and a boy called Baqt'e. A sunken log out from shore, stuck on a sand bar, would be the turn-around point, and the first to return to shore would win the race.

Djus and Baqt'e waded into the river and swam out to the log. Djus swam in the same style as Baqt'e, which was a kind of sidestroke. Once they had climbed onto the log, Djus waved.

Dauuf stood between Susan and Neferure with a piece of cloth in his hand. All the others ranged along the shore to watch the race.

Susan felt tense. She never raced at home, but this was her chance to shine at something among these people where she felt so strange. Dauuf dropped his cloth, and she and Neferure pelted across the flat for the water. Susan didn't notice Peri put her foot out, and so she tripped over her and rolled a couple of paces before she clambered to her feet again. Neferure was already in the water and swimming quite rapidly for the log.

Susan hit the water in a shallow dive and struck out strongly for Djus, who was jumping up and down and yelling to her from his perch. There was no doubt about it; her method of swimming was quicker than Neferure's. Susan gained quickly and, without much trouble, passed Neferure. By the time Susan reached the log, she was at least ten body lengths ahead of Neferure. As soon as she touched Djus's hand, he dived into the river and, swimming in the crawl, made for the shore with all speed.

Baqt'e leaned over and dived when Neferure finally touched his hand. Neferure and Susan were alone beside the log. They turned in time to see Djus clamber out of the water, jumping up and down in victory. Baqt'e still swam, only halfway back to the shore.

"You cheated," Neferure panted at her.

"Peri tripped me," Susan retorted.

"You can't swim better than me. I'm the Princess Royal."

Susan chuckled. Neferure certainly was a princess, but she didn't seem happy or confident in herself. Her eyes were angry and her mouth sulky as she glared at Susan.

"You deliberately pushed me in the mud," Susan said. "I'm glad we beat you. I'll swim rings around you any time you like. And," she added, "I won't teach you to swim like I do, either."

Susan turned to swim away.

Neferure made an ugly snarling sound deep in her throat. She reached over and grabbed Susan's youth lock and pushed her under the water. Taken by surprise, Susan gulped a mouthful of muddy river water. She struggled, but Neferure was good in the water and held her down with one hand on her shoulder. Susan tried to shake the hand loose and pulled at her youth lock. Her head felt blown up. She needed a breath, but she couldn't shake the hard little hand from her shoulder.

Her lungs burned, and desperation was close when Susan remembered her martial arts training. She was struggling against Neferure; she should be using Neferure's strength against her. With that Susan knew immediately what to do. Even though her lungs hurt and her eyes felt as though they were popping from her straining head, Susan dived. She ducked down and kicked off for the river bottom. It was a lucky kick; it connected with Neferure's side, knocking them farther apart. Susan swam as far as she could underwater and then broke the surface. Susan looked around quickly and saw that Neferure was quite a way off, coughing and spluttering in the water.

Susan floated on her back, gulping in great lungfuls of air.

In no time at all, Dauuf swam up beside her. "What happened?" he asked.

"Neferure tried to drown me," Susan spluttered angrily.

Dauuf grabbed her by the shoulders and turned her to face him. Seriously he looked deep into Susan's eyes. "Don't ever say that."

"Why not? It's true."

"True it may be, but Neferure is the Princess Royal, the daughter of Akheprerenre and his first wife, Hatshepsut. She can do no wrong—officially."

Susan saw that Dauuf was serious and realized that his advice was wise. She drew in a big breath and let it out with a sigh, trying to calm down.

"Why does Neferure hate me so much?" she asked.

"Ah, well, that's easy." Dauuf smiled. "Djus likes you so much."

The two began to sidestroke slowly to the shore.

"But why does she care? She doesn't seem to like him either, and they argue all the time."

Dauuf sighed. "Djus, Prince Useramen, is the son of Amehtu-Ahmose, who is the grand vizier for the pharaoh.

"So?" Susan rolled over onto her back and floated.

Dauuf did the same.

"For eighteen years the pharaoh had no son." Dauuf made water fountains with his hands.

"Uh-huh." Susan tried it, too.

"The grand vizier is the most important official in Egypt. He is Pharaoh's right hand. Djus is being trained to follow after his father. Neferure will have to marry someone to help her rule."

"And that someone is Djus?" Susan stared at Dauuf.

"Was Djus." Dauuf smiled and directed his water fountain at Susan's face.

"So, what changed?" Susan spluttered.

"The pharaoh, Akheperenre, had a son by a secondary wife."

"So?"

"So now, Neferure gets to marry Tuthmoses, the baby son."

Susan stopped swimming. "But aren't they brother and sister?"

Dauuf began swimming again, and Susan kept pace with him. "Yes, that's right. The baby is the heir and will be pharaoh of Egypt when his father dies—may he live for many years.

Neferure will marry the baby boy and be his great wife. She was ten years old when he was born. She would rather marry Djus."

"This is very different from the way we do things at home." Susan shook her head as she waded onto the beach.

Djus waited for her. He carried her bag and sheath in his hands. His face was set in hard lines.

"Come on," he said. "We're leaving."

Susan turned instantly toward the little reed boat. She was happy to be going. Neferure stood among her friends, and from the dark looks cast in their direction, they were ready to continue the argument.

Great, I get beheaded or something for kicking the future queen of Egypt. Just my luck, Susan thought. Djus arranged with Dauuf and Nebka to follow more slowly and bring the rest of their picnic things.

Susan and Djus pushed off quickly and set out paddling through the reeds. At first they paddled in silence, but once the picnic party on the bank disappeared from view, Djus turned the little reed boat sharply into a shallow reed bed. He pulled them far into the grove and then nosed the boat hard into a cluster of reeds. Susan could hear the wind soughing through the stiff stalks. They made a soft *shushhing* sound. Birds called back and forth, water gurgled, but there was no human sound anywhere.

"I'm sorry." Djus broke the silence.

"Why? We won, didn't we?"

Djus nodded with a smile. "Oh yes, we won, and it felt good, but I've realized that I've made Neferure very angry. You must go home immediately."

"Back to the palace?"

"No, home. Back to your country. I will ask my father to send soldiers with you to protect you. Neferure can be really nasty when she's angry."

Susan grasped the side of the boat. Home. It meant so much to her. A wave of homesickness swept over her. A hundred scenes of home flashed through her mind. Pine trees, hamburgers, her bike, French fries, her parents. Susan dipped her head so that Djus wouldn't see the sudden tears.

"I can't go home for six months." She sniffed.

"Of course you can. I will ask Pharaoh to command Harsheer to send you home."

Susan put her hand on Djus's arm. "Thanks, Djus, but it's not that simple. I cannot go home until…" *I can't tell him about the crystal growing in Pharaoh's tomb.* "Until my task here is finished."

Djus sighed. "Well, all right, but watch out for Neferure. She will be even more unfriendly now."

Hmph, he doesn't know the half of it, Susan thought ruefully. Her fingers strayed along her arm, and without thinking, she idly scratched at her mosquito bites.

Djus noticed and rummaged in his bag. He presented her with a pretty little blue pot. "Here, this will sooth the bites."

Susan gratefully smeared the cream from the pot on her arms. It felt cool and soothing.

Susan used up almost the entire pot of cream. "Thank you," she said, handing back the pot.

Djus waved it away. "You keep it. That fool of a girl of yours probably doesn't have any in store and doesn't know how to make any."

"Very possibly." Susan laughed. "She's very good at crying, sobbing, wailing, and weeping, though."

Djus nodded. "I will ask my mother to send you one of her ladies to help you. They at least are well trained."

"Well, but won't the lady mind?" she asked.

"Not at all. It will be a privilege for her to oblige," Djus retorted. "I promised to help you fit in at the palace if you taught me your method of swimming, and an honorable man always keeps his word."

"Well," Susan said gratefully, "if it's not too much trouble, it would be helpful. Most of the time, I feel like a fish flopping on the bank."

Djus laughed at the picture he had of Susan flopping in the mud on the bank of the river, and Susan joined in.

"Your land can't be that different from Egypt."

"Oh yes, it can," Susan replied mysteriously. She picked up her paddle and pushed out at the clump of reeds to end Djus's questions.

He picked up his paddle, too, and they drifted gently back to the palace in a companionable silence.

As Djus turned to leave her on the pier, he reminded Susan about meeting for the evening meal that night.

"I think I'd rather eat in my room," Susan said, thinking of the hostile looks she had received from Neferure and her friends.

Djus shook his head. "Be there," he said. "And dress like a princess," he added, laughing.

Susan looked down at her sheath. Several soakings had made it lose its pleats. It was damp at the back from the water swilling in the bottom of their little boat. Her limbs were covered in mosquito bites and mud. She was a mess.

Djus, when Susan looked, was just as dirty and messy as she. *Don't we just look like a prince and princess?* she thought, laughing to herself.

"Well, I'll have a bath anyway," she told him, laughing.

"Oh, no, tonight is going to be special," Djus informed her. "Akheperenre and I are going into Upper Egypt, and tonight is our farewell feast."

Susan was stunned. "When?"

Djus shrugged. "Tomorrow or the next day. As soon as we're ready. Akheperenre always travels to Upper Egypt at this time of the year, and he wants me to go along so I can learn all the places and meet all the nobles."

"But, but…" Susan's heart sank. The palace walls seemed to close in around her. All the twisting passageways and swarming people she didn't know. She gulped. "How long will you be gone?"

"A couple of months," Djus said. "See you tonight." He hurried off into a passageway, leaving Susan to find her way back to her own rooms.

CHAPTER 24

THE SCROLL OF MA'AT

S usan rose early from her nap. She dressed quickly and had Teo conduct her to Harsheer's rooms. She arrived just as he was climbing off his sleeping bench.

"What do you want?" he grumped, gulping water from the cup beside his bed.

Susan leaned against the wall, hoping the pose would make her look casual and relaxed. "I want to go up the river with Djus and the pharaoh."

Harsheer stood and stretched slowly and then looked across at her with a sneer. "Well, really, and how do you think you're going to manage that?"

"I…I was hoping you would help me."

"I don't want you along on the trip, getting underfoot. Saying the wrong thing. Can't even act like a princess. Stay here and learn."

Susan looked around the room and noticed that many of Harsheer's boxes and chests were packed and sealed, ready for travel.

"You're going on the trip." Susan's eyes narrowed. "I'm supposed to be your daughter. Take me, too."

"Did The One invite you?" Harsheer scratched his bare stomach.

Susan bit her lip.

"Hmph. Thought not. Run along and stop bothering me." Harsheer moved over to his workbench.

Susan hesitated, then followed him across the room. "Neferure hates me, and I'll be in danger if I stay here...alone."

"Rubbish." Harsheer waved his hands dismissively. "You're a magician and daughter of a magician. You can protect yourself." Harsheer began shoving scrolls from the table into a basket.

"Now, look," Susan said. "You have to help me. You dragged me away from my home. I helped you, and now you help me." Susan leaned over the table, trying to catch his eye. Her hand scrunched down on one of the scrolls. Looking down she noticed it was the scroll of Ma'at, the one Harsheer used to create the crystals.

Harsheer didn't answer her. He continued sorting his scrolls into the basket and began an irritating whistling sound between his teeth.

Susan's hand closed tightly around the scroll, and she slipped it off the bench and behind her back. *I hope that's your very favorite scroll—the one you really can't do without,* she thought angrily.

Susan started backing for the door.

Harsheer stopped, turned, and looked at her.

Susan froze. *Does he know I have the scroll?*

"You're a magician," Harsheer said.

Susan wrinkled up her eyes. "No, I'm not. I don't know any magic."

Harsheer smiled and held up a finger to her. "Ah, but they all believe you know magic. They all believe you're a magician. Use that. That's what most magic is."

It sounded stupid to Susan, but she nodded and backed farther toward the door, keeping the scroll behind her.

Harsheer turned as if to go back to his packing, but suddenly he looked straight at her. "Um," he asked. "Have you seen a little statue of a human figure about so big?" He held up thumb and forefinger stretched far apart."

Susan hoped he couldn't see the glow she felt. He was looking for the little statuette he had used to summon her to Egypt. The little statuette that was nestled safely in the bottom corner of her chest. "Er, no," she said casually. "What do you want it for?"

"Oh, nothing." Harsheer waved his hands and turned back to his bench, but Susan saw his shoulders slump in disappointment.

Susan put her hand to her mouth to hide her smile of triumph. She hurried out of the room and down the corridor, clutching the scroll of Ma'at to her chest.

CHAPTER 25

SUSAN'S PLAN

When Susan hurried into her room, Teo was sitting on a cushion in the corner of the room, snuffling.

With a sigh, Susan moved over to her chest and carefully placed the scroll of Ma'at in the bottom compartment with her feather, the statuette, and her green stone. Then she turned to Teo with her hands on her hips.

"Teo, would you just stop sniffling for a moment?" she said in exasperation. "You can't spend the rest of your life being miserable. At some point you just have to accept what you can't change and make the most of it."

Teo gave a big sniff and looked up into her eyes. "Is that what you do, Princess?" she asked.

And Susan nodded. She smiled as she realized that that was exactly the best way to handle all the crazy things that had happened to her—and were going to keep on happening to her.

"Come on, Teo," she said. "Cheer up." Susan looked around for something to distract the girl. "Tell you what," she said. "We're going up the river with the pharaoh and the prince tomorrow. Why don't you start packing up all the trunks and chests?"

Teo turned startled eyes on her. "But, Princess Merit-Amen, Hori told me that we…I mean…you weren't going on the journey up the river. Harsheer doesn't want you to go with him."

"Too bad for Harsheer," Susan retorted. "I want to go, and we're going. Pack up everything."

Susan saw a flash of excitement in Teo's eyes.

"Hori is going with Harsheer," Susan guessed and was rewarded with the most beautiful smile she had ever seen from Teo. Her whole face lit up.

Susan smiled, too. The whole atmosphere of the room changed with Teo's smile. Feeling lighter and more confident, Susan sat on the edge of her bed. She watched Teo, now energized and busy, moving efficiently around the room, folding and packing Susan's belongings into the chests. *I didn't realize I had so many clothes*, Susan thought as she watched.

Teo folded Susan's beautiful woolen cloak and carefully placed it in a box. Suddenly she froze and then let her hands drop to her side. Her shoulders slumped, and her head sank forward onto her chest.

Susan watched the change with a sinking feeling. "What's wrong now?"

"The Magician Prince Harsheer doesn't want you to go, so we won't go, no matter how much we might wish it," Teo whispered. Disappointment dripped from her words.

Susan felt her confidence slip, but she hung on and lifted her chin. "I am a princess here," she said loudly. "I will make this work."

Teo snuffled.

Susan rolled her eyes in disgust. "You'll see. I will work this out."

Teo looked up at her with her eyes large and round. "Oh, Princess, it would be so wonderful to be on the river with H—you," she said.

"Right. You keep packing."

Susan jumped up and hurried out the door. She had some planning to do.

Susan racked her brains. *I must get invited on that trip,* she thought. While her brain was busy, her feet led her through the palace and down to the riverbank. She sat on the end of the reed pier with her feet dangling in the water. The pier bobbed gently with the movement of the water, and the lowering sun shone red in her face.

Her eyes took in the scene around her. The flooded river surged around her feet. Small children laughed and splashed in the shallows. Women carried large jars to the water's edge, where they stooped to fill them from the river. Laughing and calling to one another, they lifted the jars to their heads and walked back toward the houses.

The river itself was busy with small reed boats, and as she watched, a large wooden boat swept up to the pier. The boat was painted with gold, and the fine linen that hung over the little cabin was decorated with strings of colored beads that rattled gently in the breeze. *I guess this is the pharaoh's boat*, she thought.

Servants began moving chests and trunks onto the boat as soon as it was firmly tied to the pier. Other boats drew alongside, too, and these were loaded even higher with all the goods and food required to take a pharaoh and his followers on a trip up the river.

Susan thought of the river that flowed near her home. She thought of the way the clear, cold water rippled and sparkled over the pebbles; how she could see right into the water; and how the tall pines sheltered the river from the sun. She thought of snow falling and hissing into the river. It was all so different. How would anyone at home ever believe what was happening to her?

And then she had it. How would anyone here ever believe what her home was like? *It will all seem like stories to them*, she realized. *Anything I tell them about my home will seem like a wonderful story to them.*

Susan jumped to her feet and hurried back to her rooms.

As she neared the door, Susan heard a faint singing. She put her ear to the door, and sure enough, Teo was singing to herself.

Susan pushed the door open and saw Teo busily packing and looking the happiest she had ever been.

Teo turned to Susan and smiled. "I can tell by your face that you have thought of a plan, Princess."

"Well, yes," Susan said, "I think it will work."

Teo sighed happily. "I knew you would."

Susan hid the fact that she didn't feel as confident as Teo. It boosted her spirits to have someone else so sure of her. She straightened her shoulders.

"Teo," she said. "Make me the grandest, most beautiful princess in the land." She practiced a gesture that she thought a storyteller might use.

Teo actually chuckled. "I can, Princess," she said. "The lady Miew from the grand vizier's household came and showed me a lot of things that will help."

Ah, Djus kept his promise. Susan smiled.

They ripped into the boxes and pulled out all the jewelry and clothing—again.

They spent ages painting Susan's face just so.

Finally they were done. Susan peered into her look-face and an Egyptian princess looked back at her. She laughed with pleasure, and Teo joined in.

They had both had such fun dressing her up that Susan's eyes sparkled with excitement. She pulled her head up even higher. She straightened her shoulders and sailed out the door. As she turned the corner at the end of the passage, she could faintly hear Teo humming to herself in their room.

Susan walked along the corridor to the feast.

Susan hesitated in the doorway to the courtyard. There were many people already sitting around the little tables dotted across the floor. Music and muttering spilled out to where she stood. The smell of flowers and spicy food wafted on the gentle breeze. Her stomach turned over, and she looked longingly back down the corridor. It would be so easy to sneak back to her room, but she squared her shoulders and marched across the threshold.

"*The princess Merit-Amen.*"

Susan lifted her chin high and walked into the crowd.

She moved toward the pharaoh and queen, who were sitting on their chairs at the cooler end of the courtyard. She bowed very low.

"Ah, Merit-Amen." The pharaoh smiled at her in a slightly vague way.

"Merit-Amen? Ah, yes," Queen Hatshepsut cut in, "the swimmer." The queen's voice was the coldest thing Susan had encountered since arriving in Egypt.

Looking into her icy eyes, Susan quailed inwardly. She quickly turned her attention to the pharaoh.

"Great One," she started hesitantly, "I have enjoyed my stay in your palace greatly."

The pharaoh nodded to her. Susan noticed a twinkle deep in his eyes, and this gave her the courage to continue.

"I would like to see more of your great land while I am here."

Susan heard Hatshepsut's sharp intake of breath.

"I would like to accompany you on your trip up the river," she hurried on. "I…I have many wonderful tales to tell of my land and of people and animals that are wondrous to behold." She waved her hand in an expansive gesture.

"That's ridiculous," Hatshepsut cut in. "You're dragging Useramen along instead of taking his father, the true vizier. Now you're going to take this upstart princess as well. You know that I am totally capable of ruling here while you are gone. Take Amehtu-Ahmose with you instead."

Akheperenre turned and looked at his queen slowly. "How interesting," he drawled.

"Then Neferure should go, too," Hatshepsut added sharply.

Akheperenre looked about to protest, but before he could speak, Harsheer presented himself. He bowed low and rubbed his hands in front of him.

"Oh, Great One," he intoned, "this daughter is disobedient. Please forgive her presumption. Of course, you won't want her on the river with us. She knows nothing. She is ignorant." Harsheer turned a sneering face to her. "She gets in the way."

Susan's heart sank. How could she argue with these people? She hung her head and turned to leave, but a gentle voice, barely above a whisper, stopped her.

"Merit-Amen?" She faced the pharaoh, and he beckoned her forward. "Will you teach me to swim as well as you?" he whispered in her ear.

Susan pulled back to look into his eyes to gauge whether he was serious or just teasing her. She saw a twinkle in his eye, and taking a deep breath, she said, "It would be my pleasure, oh, Great One."

Susan bowed deeply.

The pharaoh laughed out loud and clapped his hands together. "That's settled then." He stood and announced in a large voice, "The Princess Merit-Amen accompanies us on the river tomorrow."

There was a sudden hush in the courtyard. Susan felt that everyone was staring at her. She wanted to curl up small, but she pulled her shoulders straight instead. She turned and found Djus standing at her elbow, grinning from ear to ear. The two of them bowed low to the pharaoh and to the queen. Then they slipped across the courtyard to the table where Nebka and Dauuf sat waiting for them.

The meal was almost over, and Susan was close to sleep before she noticed Neferure. She was sitting at a table on the other side of the courtyard. Her friends were gathered around her, their heads close together. They were talking rapidly. At one point Neferure looked up, and her eyes caught on Susan's. The look Susan saw in their depths made her shiver.

When Susan awoke the next morning, Teo was not in the room. All the boxes and chests were packed and all the bundles were tied, but Teo was nowhere to be found.

I suppose she's already gone ahead to the boat, Susan thought.

She found a fresh sheath lying on the end of her bed, and her beautiful cloak was laid out as well, so Susan quickly dressed. She felt excited about the day. Susan took great gulps of fresh air into her lungs. *I am going to travel up the Nile with the pharaoh.* Susan hugged herself. *I am the friend of the grand vizier's son.*

I will see such wonders. We'll have great adventures. Susan twirled on the spot.

She was tying her sandals when Hori entered the room.

"Princess." He smiled, bowed to her, and picked up one of her storage chests and left. Other soldiers followed him, and soon all Susan's chests and bundles were carried off and the room lay empty.

Susan hurried after them; she didn't want to miss the boat.

The air was chilly, and she hugged her cloak around her as she hurried along. Mist drifted off the water. Everything was quiet. The sky was light, but as of yet the sun hadn't risen over the horizon behind the city.

Susan paused on the bank of the river and drew in a deep breath. The day smelled fresh and clean. With a laugh, she hurried excitedly down to the waiting boats.

CHAPTER 26

ON THE RIVER AGAIN

S usan took a deep breath of the fresh morning air. She stood right in the front of the boat. There she could watch the water split and ripple along the sides. This was her favorite place.

For two weeks they had sailed in a leisurely fashion up the river. Every night they stopped at the home of a governor or entered the precincts of one of the many temples that jutted on the high ground above the river.

Teaching Pharaoh to swim was no chore at all. He quickly mastered the leg and arm movements, and with Susan and Djus swimming along with him, he had soon mastered the correct breathing as well. Away from the large boat, with soldiers around them to ensure there were no crocodiles in the water, they splashed and played in the river shallows. It was easy to forget that Tuthmoses II was also Akheperenre the pharaoh.

In their time on the river, Susan had grown used to acting the princess. She could wave and smile, and she could look haughtily down her nose when that seemed the right attitude to strike. After the first week, she decided that she liked being a princess and had quickly learned to be good at it. She had grown used to the clothing—or lack of it—and could now carry herself comfortably while bedecked in so much jewelry that she rattled when she walked. She still liked the bells woven into her youth lock. Many wore wigs on formal occasions, but Susan found she preferred the freedom of her youth lock.

This very morning they had left a governor's palace early. The mist still drifted on the wind blowing up the river; the wind filled the sails of the boats. The cliffs to the west of the river were already aflame in the early sunrise, but on the river itself, the air still held a little chill.

I guess I've been here about a month now, Susan thought as she peered ahead of the boat to see what the next wonder would be. *Five more to go.*

Egypt was a wonderful place, and Susan had learned to love it. Except for the nagging and continuous pull of homesickness, she would be happy.

She bit her lip. She felt a little as though she had betrayed her family in some way.

The trip on the river had shown her many different aspects of the land. She saw the granaries built on the high ground. She saw people working to shore up the dykes that kept the flooding river away from their homes. At every town and temple along the way, the people rushed to the river's edge to cheer and wave as the boat carrying their pharaoh sailed by. They seemed, to Susan, to be a happy people.

They entered the temples to the sound of chanting and singing. The pharaoh brought fruit and chickens, which he laid on the altar. Everyone brought something.

In some of the temples, acolytes pushed open huge doors to admit the priests and just the pharaoh into inner secret places. Then the rest of the party waited outside. Often Djus went into the inner sanctum with Harsheer and the pharaoh.

Egypt had many gods, all different and amazing to Susan. Most of the gods seemed to have an animal personality as well. She learned about Horus and how he appeared as a hawk. She understood better why the feather drifting into her hand had seemed so important to the men who had found her when she first arrived.

There seemed to be a god or goddess for everything; to look after every aspect of life.

When the pharaoh appeared again, coming out through the imposing temple doors into the blinding light, Susan understood why the people could see him as a god. Susan was glad she knew the other Akheperenre. The man who laughed at jokes and got tipsy at parties. The man whose eyes twinkled when he looked at her. The man who held his kingship so lightly that he could be a friend one minute and a pharaoh the next and then come through a door and appear to his people as a god.

Susan took another deep breath and turned from the bow of the boat to walk back into the shade of the awning erected for their comfort. Throwing herself onto the cushions, she sipped at the cool drink Teo handed her. Just forward of her position, she saw Harsheer. He and the pharaoh sat with their heads close together, talking and planning.

A sigh escaped from Susan as she handed the empty mug back to Teo. Harsheer still worried her. *I don't trust him.* He had made her his daughter for his own reasons, and he didn't have her best interests at heart, she was sure. *I will have to watch when the six months is up. He might sneak back to Akheperenre's tomb and take all the crystals for himself,* she thought. He seemed an ambitious man, cold and calculating.

"Merit-Amen."

Susan sat up from the cushions.

Djus's head showed above the edge of the boat. He must have been in his reed canoe alongside. Susan jumped up and hurried over.

"Come on, Merit-Amen. Come paddling with me," he invited.

Susan quickly clambered over the side into the little reed boat, and taking up the second paddle, she dug into the water with a will.

Working together they pulled ahead of the slower, lumbering boats sailing up the river on the gentle wind. They angled for the shore to rest in the shade of the flooded palms.

Workmen were standing knee-deep in the ooze near their resting place. When Susan and Djus first arrived, all stopped work and bowed deeply to the pair. But Djus nonchalantly waved them back to work, and they soon became busy again.

Susan watched, fascinated. The men scooped up buckets of river mud and passed them to others working on the shore. These men sloshed the mud into wooden boxes and mixed in handfuls of straw and some little pebbles. Water slopped out over the top and also drained out through holes near the bottom of the box.

Once all the water had drained away, the men turned the boxes upside down and tipped out squares of mud, which they set in the sun to dry.

"What are those men doing?" Susan asked.

Djus looked over lazily. "They're making bricks," he replied.

"Bricks? To build houses, you mean?"

Djus nodded. "The Nile will start receding soon, and then there will be many bricks needed to repair the damage caused by the floods."

"But what happens when they get wet in the floods?"

"They dissolve. That's why we make more for when the flood recedes," Djus explained slowly.

"All right, all right." Susan laughed. "So you know it's different where I'm from." She had told Djus and the pharaoh quite a bit about her home on the slow trip up the river. "What happens when it rains, though?" Susan asked.

"What rain?" Djus shrugged.

"Water falls from the sky when it rains. Big, cold drops of water splashing down everywhere."

Djus shrugged again. "That doesn't happen very often here. You don't have to worry."

But now Susan was thinking of home. "Sometimes it's so cold that the rain comes down as snow and lays all over the ground in great mounds that you can climb up and slide down."

"Water goes up in mounds and stays there." Djus pulled a wry face. "Yes, Merit-Amen, and sand gets so hot it turns into glass," he retorted.

Djus picked up his paddle at that moment because the royal boat had caught up to them.

Susan did the same. *I don't think he believes me about rain and snow,* she thought. *It's just another one of my fantastic stories, like the one about the carriage that goes without horses and the lights that brighten the night without flame.* Susan chuckled to herself.

They clambered on board Pharaoh's boat and then quickly pulled the reed boat out of the water and fitted it into its storage spot in the stern. They all slept during the heat of the day while the boat sailed gently south along the endless river.

CHAPTER 27

THE TEMPLE OF MA'AT

When Susan awoke, the boats were tied to the shore in the shadow of a small temple. As she pushed out through the drifting curtains, she could see that almost everyone was still asleep. She dipped herself a mug of water from the crock standing in the shade of the sail and moved to the front of the boat, sipping as she went.

The temple was smaller than most they had visited, but the areas around the central courtyard were bright and beautiful with myriad flowers growing in pots. Susan saw chrysanthemums in bright yellow and orange, and red poppies bobbed their heads in a gentle breeze. Trees grew in a grove beside the temple, and the shade they offered immediately tempted Susan. She climbed off the boat and hurried into the shelter of the branches.

As soon as she entered the grove, she felt her heart lifting. Throwing her arms wide, she twirled around in the cool, slightly tangy air. She loved the soft shushing noise the leaves made in the breeze. She drew in a deep breath; the trees made the air smell fresh. *Not like the burned dirt smell of the desert,* she thought, leaning against a scratchy tree trunk.

The next tree into the grove had a low-hanging branch. Susan couldn't resist it. Grabbing hold she swung up into the branches. One led to another as though the tree offered her a staircase. Soon she pulled herself onto a high branch, which offered her a perch. The leaves closed around her. It was heaven. *This feels more like home than anywhere else I've been in Egypt,* she thought.

The tree grew spindly twigs out from the branches, and each twig was thickly covered with shiny green leaves. The undersides were a deep silver color. Susan found that the twigs pulled off easily into her hands, and that, because they were supple, she could weave the strands into a circlet. It felt almost as though the twigs were doing the work themselves, they wove together so readily. It could have taken a minute or it could have taken an hour. Susan wove the strands together, totally absorbed in her task.

When the circlet was complete, she had a ring thickly covered with glossy leaves. She fitted it to her head, and it sat there like a cap of shiny green. She pulled her youth lock through the hole in the side, and the circlet settled gently on her head. The leaves felt refreshingly cool on her skin.

Boom. Boom. Susan started up to listen to the deep drum beat. It was the parade drum from the boat. She was late.

She hurried out of the tree and ran through the grove toward the temple. She hoped to slip onto the end of the line so nobody would notice her absence.

Harsheer grabbed her youth lock and pulled her to a stop. "You're late," he snarled. "You've been in the sacred grove."

Susan pulled her lock from his hands and glared.

"Nobody but the initiated may enter the sacred grove of Ma'at, you stupid girl." He shook her. "You'll be in trouble with the priestess."

Susan pulled free from him and hurried to catch up with the end of the line. How was she supposed to know it was a sacred grove? She hadn't seen any signs saying, "keep out."

Everyone was assembled in the courtyard when she arrived. She slipped in and stood half-hidden behind Djus. She peeped out around his shoulder.

Akheperenre stood alone before the priestesses. He bowed to them. Susan had never seen him bow so low to any priests or priestesses before, even in the largest temples. *Whose temple is this?* Susan wondered. *Ma'at, Harsheer said. Why does that name sound so familiar?*

Someone struck a temple gong. The sound reverberated around the courtyard. Everyone bowed low, including Susan, and as she did, she remembered. The scroll of Ma'at. The crystals of Ma'at. This temple had something to do with her crystal. She stood up to get a better look around—and stood face-to-face with the high priestess. Everyone else still bowed low; only Susan and the priestesses stood.

The high priestess turned her expressionless eyes on Susan and crooked her finger. *She wants me to follow her.* Susan gulped and hung back. Harsheer pushed her out of line.

"You desecrated the sacred grove, you'll be punished," he gloated in her ear.

The other priestesses formed a tight group around her, and they followed after the high priestess. Susan had no option but to walk along with them. Her eyes scanned the crowd as she hustled along with the priestesses. Djus looked alarmed, but Akheperenre smiled at her.

The large double doors at the end of the courtyard shut behind her with a decisive bang. The noise echoed through the large room.

The women relaxed immediately. Soft cushions covered the floor and fruits and wine from the temple offerings sat on a small table. The priestesses led Susan to a cushion and then arranged themselves on cushions around her. They looked at her expectantly. Susan played with her fingers in her lap. She kept her head down and watched the women through her lashes. This wasn't what she had expected at all.

"Welcome to our home, Chosen of Ma'at." The high priestess spoke to her. Susan was surprised at the words.

"I'm sorry," she said. "I didn't know the grove was sacred. I didn't mean any harm."

The women laughed, a tinkle of merriment that made Susan feel a lot more confident. She looked up to see that everyone was smiling at her.

"Oh, Crystal Bearer." The high priestess laughed. "You are always welcome anywhere in a temple of Ma'at. You are of her chosen and may come and go in any temple of Ma'at as you please." The woman leaned back in her cushions. "And as for the grove," she added, "Harsheer would have had an unpleasant experience if he had entered."

Susan touched the cap of leaves that sat on her head. "He waited for me outside the grove."

"Of course he did." The priestess nodded. "He has used the scroll of Ma'at against her wishes. He is proud and arrogant and steps very lightly around this temple for fear that Ma'at will strike him down in anger."

"Because he's growing the crystals of Ma'at?" Susan asked.

The priestess waved her hand dismissively. "We were concerned about his magic doings. We don't know how he acquired the scroll he used. We made sure he always failed." The tray of drinks was passed to Susan. She took one and passed the tray on.

The priestess continued, "But then he summoned you to help him, and you've restored the balance. There was no need for us to interfere. Ma'at will be served."

Susan needed to learn a lot more about what was happening. "But…But how will I get home?" she blurted out. She had a million questions to ask.

The priestess smiled and stroked her arm gently. "It will be as Ma'at requires," she said. The women stood again, straightening their robes. They lined up facing the door, only this time Susan stood beside the high priestess.

The woman took down a box that stood on a pillar beside the massive doors. She opened it and pulled from its depths a necklace. She held it up for all to see. The pendant was suspended on an intricately braided linen cord. The pendant, which was larger than Susan's hand, showed a woman, kneeling, her arms outstretched. Feathers lined the length of her arms and one long feather stuck up from the top of her head. Her face smiled in the silver. Colored glass was fused to the silver so that the pendant glowed with reds, blues, and greens.

Susan reached out a tentative finger and stroked the beautiful pendant.

"Ma'at?" she asked. The high priestess nodded, smiling, and dropped the pendant around Susan's neck. The weight of the piece thumped against her chest, but Susan liked the feel of it.

The priestess kissed her on both cheeks. "You belong to Ma'at," she said. Then she kissed Susan on the top of her head. "Ma'at belongs to you." She held Susan away from her and smiled into her eyes.

The huge gong sounded again, and the doors swung open. Susan walked proudly out into the courtyard. All bowed. Susan took a deep breath and held it. *I belong*, she thought.

Harsheer hissed through his teeth and stalked from the courtyard. The others clustered around her in congratulations. They all moved back to the boat in a skipping, hopping group.

Susan had one chance to talk to the high priestess again. She touched her arm and pulled her aside. "I need to learn more about Ma'at," Susan said.

The priestess patted her arm and smiled knowingly. "You have the scroll of Ma'at. Read it. It's all there." She laughed at the way Susan's eyes grew large.

How did she know I had the scroll? Susan wondered.

CHAPTER 28

WHAT IS A MENAGERIE?

S usan stood in the bow of the boat as it rounded a river bend and the next town came into view. The palace of the local governor rose up over the town and the Nile. Townspeople and the palace servants bustled about. *Last-minute preparations*, Susan thought with a smile.

A trumpet blew to announce their arrival.

People rushed down the steep bank, excitedly pushing and shoving to get a glimpse of Akheperenre. Susan loved to watch the excitement; it always seemed friendly to her. The people seemed so eager to see their pharaoh and to be in his presence.

"Princess Merit-Amen," an amused voice called her. She turned, startled, and saw everyone ready to leave the boat. Akheperenre beckoned. They were waiting for her.

She quickly ran to take her place beside Harsheer. "Can't you ever do anything right?" he snarled.

Akheperenre turned to Susan. "Walk with me, child," he ordered.

Susan quickly ran forward in the line and stood beside the pharaoh. Djus stood on the other side and leaned forward and winked at her as she settled into place.

Akheperenre chuckled. "Well, here we go again." He sighed and signaled to his trumpeters.

At a loud blast, all the people on the shore fell quiet. All the pushing and shoving stopped. Akheperenre threw his arms around the shoulders of Djus and Susan, and the three stepped onto the gangplank and walked ashore. The others followed.

A long reed mat stretched over the mud, and they walked easily through the throng. People pressed flowers into their hands as they passed. At the top of the bank, the governor of the province awaited them. He bowed deeply as they approached.

"Up, up," Akheperenre insisted. "Not you, Pawara, never you, my oldest friend." Pharaoh wrapped the governor in a firm embrace. The governor, Pawara, relaxed, laughed, and slapped Pharaoh on the back.

The crowd gasped, but Pharaoh laughed and slapped Pawara's back in turn.

Susan watched Akheperenre, the Great One, turn into Tuthmoses, the friend, right there in front of her.

"Tell me about the menagerie. Have we any new animals? What creatures can you show me?" Tuthmoses paced in a little circle.

Pawara laughed. He was a young man, agile and quick on his feet. He waved his hand in a beckoning gesture. He and the pharaoh were of a height. It was obvious to Susan that the governor and the pharaoh were close friends.

"Come and see," Pawara said.

They hurried off together without another thought for the people trailing along behind.

"Hmmph." Harsheer sniffed, drawing alongside Susan. "You think he favors you, but it is nothing. He didn't present you to the governor or anything. All he cares about is his precious menagerie."

Djus overheard Harsheer's words and turned glaring eyes on him. "Have a care, old man," he threatened. "You may be the chief priest of Re and the court magician, but not even you can show such spite."

Harsheer drew himself up to his full height and stared down at Djus. He made finger passes in Djus's direction. "You're not vizier yet, little Useramen," he said. He turned on his heel. "Come, Merit-Amen, attend me," he snapped, as he stalked away.

Great, thought Susan, *this is going to be fun.* She slowly turned to follow, but Djus caught her arm.

"Come on," he said. "We're going to the menagerie, too."

Susan laughed. "What's a menagerie?" *It couldn't be worse than spending time with a grumpy Harsheer.* The two hurried after the two friends.

"I've never seen the Great One so relaxed with a governor anywhere during our trip," Susan observed.

"Tuthmoses and Pawara grew up together in the palace." Djus paced alongside Susan.

"Tuthmoses had two older brothers, and so he was never expected to be the next pharaoh," Djus continued.

Susan stopped by a pool to admire the fish swimming within. Djus stood beside her.

"What happened to the older brothers?" she wanted to know.

"The oldest was Amenmose." Djus counted them off on his fingers. "He was a great warrior and was named Great Overseer of Soldiers. He was courageous and daring, and one day, while hunting ibex in the desert, he smashed his chariot over a boulder." Djus shook his head.

"So, he smashed his chariot…" Susan encouraged him.

"He rolled free and got up laughing. Nobody thought anything of it until he fell asleep and could not be awakened." Djus sighed. "That's when they found the big lump on the back of his head. He had obviously hit his head on a rock when he fell." Djus shrugged. "The physicians tried everything, but nothing worked. He died."

Djus knelt beside the pond and wiggled his fingers in the water. The fish came.

"And the other brother?" Susan prodded.

Djus started. "Oh yes, Wadjmose. He sickened and died quite young. Nobody was sure why."

Susan looked up and noticed that the others were way ahead of them.

They hurried to catch up with Tuthmoses and Pawara.

"When Tuthmoses first became pharaoh, the tribes of Nubia rebelled," Djus continued. The two trailed Tuthmoses and Pawara through an arch set in the wall at the bottom of the formal palace gardens.

"Pawara led the armies to the south and subdued the tribes again. He is quite young to be a governor but he has kept the region peaceful and prosperous. He keeps our southern borders safe for Egypt."

"Djus, you are starting to sound like a vizier yourself." Susan poked him in the ribs. "You know all the history and the goings-on."

Djus shrugged. "That's my training. It's my duty to keep Egypt safe and prosperous, and to serve my pharaoh."

Susan turned to follow along the path. She quickly saw that the menagerie was a small zoo. In one corner of the estate of the governor's palace, there were pens and stables with a large variety of animals in them. They caught up with Tuthmoses standing by a pen. Inside stood a beautiful, delicate deer. She had two fawns with her. The pharaoh and the governor were chatting happily about the correct type of feed for her while peering through the stakes that kept the deer enclosed.

The next pen contained a crocodile. It lay perfectly still in a pond made especially for it. Its nostrils, eyes, and a small part of its back were all Susan could see above the water. Tuthmoses leaned on the top of the wall, peering closely at the crocodile. Susan leaned on the wall, too, and noticed it was built of the mud bricks she had seen the workmen making along the riverbank.

I hope the water doesn't slosh out of his pond and wash away the wall, she thought, rubbing her finger on the hardened mud surface.

In the corner of the garden stood a high wall. Pawara conducted them across the grass and gestured proudly. On three sides, the enclosure reached at least ten feet high, but on the side where they stood, the wall only came to their waists.

Susan rested her hand on the wall but pulled it away quickly. Her fingers were slightly muddy. *This wall must be very new.*

Several trees grew in the space, but most of the area was flat and dusty. A pond occupied one corner. *What's in here?* A branch ripped off one of the trees, and a creature ambled out into the open, the branch firmly grasped in its trunk.

"An elephant," Susan exclaimed.

They all looked at her in surprise. "You know about elephants?" The governor seemed disappointed. "But it only arrived two days ago. We hurried to have it here for Tuthmoses's visit."

"Well,…well…" Susan wasn't sure how much to say.

"Ah, our Princess Merit-Amen knows many strange and wonderful things. She delights us with her tales of other places." Pharaoh beamed down at her.

The governor bowed with a flourish. "I look forward to hearing these wondrous tales," he said with a smile. The two adults returned to their conversation about elephants and how this one was caught and how large the tusks were, and the long journey over land it had taken to bring it to this place.

Djus and Susan wandered off.

The next enclosure held a cheetah. It lay on its side on the top of a large rock in the center of the enclosure. Only the tip of its tail moved.

"Sometimes they can be trained to hunt with the soldiers," Djus told her. "Maybe they are training this one."

"It doesn't look trained to me." Susan watched the cheetah slowly blink at her. She could hear the low, grumbling noise it made.

"No, it doesn't look tame at all," Djus agreed as they turned to leave.

CHAPTER 29

AN HONOR NECKLACE

The feast that night was a festive affair. Akheperenre and the governor sat in chairs on a
dais at one end of the courtyard. As soon as Susan
entered the courtyard, the crowd fell silent. Everyone watched her walk across the dining area to sit at
the table with Djus. All through the evening, people
came to their table. They would sit awhile and chat
before moving on. Several reached out and touched
the pendant of Ma'at that Susan wore. They smiled
and bobbed their heads to her.

In a quiet time when only Djus and Susan were
sitting at the table, she asked him what was so special about Ma'at and the pendant. Djus explained to
her that the pendent marked her as one of Ma'at's

chosen, and that the goddess Ma'at oversaw balance. She was the goddess who stood for truth and justice.

"Ma'at keeps chaos at bay," Djus said as if that explained everything.

Djus told her that when Egyptians died, their hearts were put onto a scale and weighed against the feather of Ma'at. Looking at the pendant, Susan could see the feather Ma'at wore it in her hair. The people who had hearts heavier than the feather did not travel to the field of reeds in the west. The field of reeds was a wonderful place where the river teemed with game and the grain grew waist high, where flowers decked the trees and life was blissful.

Sounds like heaven, Susan thought.

A trumpet sounded. Harsheer entered the feasting area. He scowled at Susan as he stomped by on his way up to the chairs occupied by Akheperenre and Pawara. He held out a large bag toward Pharaoh. From the way he carried it, Susan could guess that the bag was quite heavy.

Akheperenre stood. Thrusting his hand into the bag, he turned to Pawara. "Stand," he ordered.

Pawara stood. Just a little unsure.

Akheperenre pulled a necklet of golden beads from the bag. He slipped it over Pawara's head. "I honor you for your service," he said.

Everyone in the room began gently knocking their wine cups on the table. It was a kind of clapping.

Susan joined in.

Djus leaned toward her. "Pharaoh is truly honoring Pawara," he whispered. "That golden necklace makes Pawara a wealthy man. More important, though, everyone will know that he is honored and valued by the pharaoh Akheperenre."

Akheperenre held up his hand for silence. He turned.

"Princess Merit-Amen." He beckoned to Susan.

She stood shakily and moved to his side.

"You have been with us only a short time," he said. "You have brought new skills and new tales to our court." He reached into the bag and pulled out another necklace, a little smaller than the one given to Pawara, and dropped it over her head. The beads were cool against her skin. Hanging around her neck, the necklet drooped below the pendant of Ma'at. It was very heavy.

Susan looked up into Pharaoh's laughing eyes. "Thank you," she said. She bowed low and then straightened. "You honor me, Great Pharaoh."

Akheperenre patted her shoulder and gave her a gentle push back toward her seating cushions.

She sat. She lifted the weight of the necklet into her hands. Each bead was shaped and decorated. Susan saw bees and tiny flower buds. She ran her fingers over a tiny golden almond. It was a lovely thing.

She looked up and noticed that Harsheer was standing to one side. He was furious.

After the feast Susan slipped out into the garden. The full moon shone through a few drifting clouds, and the light made it easy for Susan to see her way. It was cool and fresh in the night air. The last revelers from the feast were still laughing and singing in the courtyard, but the garden was quiet.

She lifted the weight of the honor necklet and bounced it on her hand. Such an honor. Susan had attended other presentations of honor necklets at the palace, but she had never expected to receive one of her own. Two wonderful necklets she owned now. Neither had anything to do with Harsheer. They were hers.

As she wandered along the paths, Susan ran her fingers over the pendent of Ma'at. *Of course,* she thought, *Mrs. Coleman told me that we travel to restore the balance of things. My crystal must be one of these crystals of Ma'at. That means that it must grow and I must get it because in the future I have it. But wait, what if my coming back here has changed all that.* Susan's mind worried round and round. What if…What might happen… Why me?

Susan shuddered. She was cold. Surprised, she noticed the moon no longer shone down into the garden, and looking up, she saw clouds covering the sky. Susan sniffed the air. It smelled damp. *I suppose there might be dew tomorrow,* she thought as she hurried inside.

CHAPTER 30

RAIN

Susan woke when cool water dripped onto her shoulder. She rolled over and sat up. Her bed-sheet was wet. Rain. She could hear it pattering down outside. Susan drew a deep breathe. She could smell it. So fresh.

Another drip fell, this time on her head.

She jumped up, laughing. Her feet splashed in the water on the floor, and water trickled and dripped down the walls. She rummaged for her sheath.

"Teo," she whispered, "get up. It's raining."

Teo stirred.

Susan shook her shoulder. "Get up, Teo. It's raining."

Teo sat up with a squeal. "Raining, Princess?"

"Yes, you know, water falls from the sky."

"Water flows in the Great River, Princess," Teo said with certainty as she rolled off her pallet.

"OK, OK," Susan agreed, tugging at her arm, "come outside and see."

Susan hurried along the passageway with Teo stumbling along behind. The passage was a puddle as the rain splashed in through the opening under the roof. *Looks like the roof is leaking, too.*

Closer to the outside doorway, Susan heard the rain beating down. It sounded wonderful to her. She pushed the door open, smiling happily—and stepped out into a sea of mud.

Mud oozed up through her toes. The rain fell so hard that each drop splashed up a fountain of mud. The sound was deafening.

Teo squealed and huddled back into the doorway, but Susan ran out into the courtyard with her arms spread wide. She turned her face up and let the warm rain beat down on her. She stood, drinking in the smell, sound, and taste of rain. *I'll never complain about rain again.*

Susan felt Teo tugging at her arm. Teo was crying again.

"What is it this time?" Susan asked.

"Oh, Princess," Teo gasped, "please come inside. This is dangerous. The gods must be very angry. It never rains like this in Egypt."

"You go. I'm staying." Laughing, Susan stamped her foot, spraying mud all over Teo and herself.

Susan told Teo, "You go inside and move our chests onto the bed to keep them dry. I don't want my ceremonial cape to get wet."

Susan followed the path through the garden. Water rushed along the pathway, turning it into a small stream. As she approached the arch, it began to creak and move. Susan watched in horror as the arch bent toward her almost as though bowing. She darted back just in time to avoid being struck by the falling gateway. It crashed down with a huge splash, sending mud spraying in all directions. *I guess the rushing water weakened the foundations.*

Susan ran forward and climbed over the mess. What had been a sturdy gateway was now a heap of straw, sticks, and running mud. The rain teemed down. The archway was being washed away before her eyes. *Sun-dried mud bricks aren't meant for heavy rain*, she realized.

Crrrrash. Something else fell. Susan jumped up and hurried toward the menagerie. She looked back nervously at the wall. *What will fall next?* she wondered.

All the governor's soldiers and the pharaoh's were running through the rain. All the palace servants also scurried about. Some carried children and women into the main buildings, which were made of stone. Others stumbled along under loads of chests and furniture.

Even if the roof leaks and the floors are wet, the stone buildings won't fall, Susan realized.

Most of the activity seemed to be centered on the menagerie. Susan found Djus by the animal pens. He was digging a trench, trying to drain off the water that was pooling at the foot of a low wall. She grabbed a stick and helped him gouge a channel to draw the water away.

Working together, they soon had a groove dug, and the puddle began to drain. Djus and Susan leaned against the wall to rest. It was soft and felt spongy. They stood instead.

"The gods must be angry," Djus said, shaking his head. "What could we have done?"

"Gods nothing," Susan replied. "It's only rain. It rains like this all the time where I come from." *Of course, it doesn't wash our walls away,* she added to herself, looking around.

"How can you stand it?" Djus wanted to know.

Susan opened her mouth to explain about her home, but it was just too different. She shrugged instead and turned away. Her foot slipped in the mud, and she fell heavily against Djus. Neither could regain their balance, and slipping and sliding, the two of them fell heavily against the little wall. The wall swayed and buckled and then sagged away under them. The two fell into the animal pen in a muddy heap.

Susan felt Djus go rigid.

"Don't move," he whispered urgently in her ear.

Susan heard it—the hiss of a crocodile. She could smell the carrion smell, and she knew which animal pen they were in.

Susan lay in the mud, wishing she could just dissolve away like the mud bricks. She couldn't even see the crocodile from her position. Then, over the sound of the driving rain, Susan heard the scrape of the crocodile's scales on the ground. He approached them slowly. The two froze.

The crocodile came closer still. Susan felt its breath on her neck. She tried to think herself invisible.

Then, in a sudden flurry, the crocodile rushed for the hole in the fence. It ran right along Susan's side. Its scales scraped her back, and its swinging tail gave her a sharp whack as it ran by to freedom.

Susan still couldn't move, she was so shaken. Djus shook her shoulder and sat her upright.

"Merit-Amen, are you all right?"

Susan shook her head.

"Come on. We have to tell Akheperenre that the crocodile is loose."

Susan climbed reluctantly to her feet, and the two of them set off, slipping and sliding, gripping each other for support.

Many of the pen walls had fallen. Susan saw the deer wander by, followed by one fawn. Susan had no time to worry about the other one. They hurried on.

The two found the two friends, Tuthmoses and Pawara, by the elephant pen. Harsheer stood to one side, keening into the falling water. His singsong added to the general noise.

I suppose he's going to tell everyone that he stopped the rain with his chanting, Susan thought sourly.

The soldiers were organized into lines. One line scooped up the mud and handed it to the other line, which piled it onto the front wall of the elephant pen. As fast as the rain washed it away, they piled it back on the wall.

The elephant paced restlessly in its enclosure. His head swung nervously from side to side, his trunk up, questing the air.

Susan saw Pharaoh rush along the wall shouting at the men. He stopped and peered anxiously over the wall at the elephant.

Susan spotted a sudden movement in the corner of her eye, and turning quickly, she saw the cheetah leap onto the crumbling wall. It was soaked through, and its tail twitched angrily.

"Djus"—she grabbed his arm—"the cheetah has escaped."

The bedraggled cheetah lashed out at a workman. Three long gashes appeared on the man's arm. He let out a frightened scream and fell back into the mud. The cheetah turned nervously on the wall, which crumbled under its feet. It let out a yowl of misery and frustration.

The elephant went rigid, its big ears pricked to the sound.

The cheetah yowled again. It moaned low its throat and fell forward into the elephant's pen. With a frustrated hiss, the cheetah gathered its feet under itself and sprang straight for the elephant.

In a flash the elephant ran. It let out one long, thin scream of its own and lumbered at the crumbling fence. Pawara, seeing his precious elephant ready to escape, ran forward, waving his arms to stop it.

The elephant, in its panic, tossed its head, catching Pawara on its tusk. Pawara screamed once as the elephant threw him off to the side, his chest horribly mangled.

Tuthmoses ran toward his friend.

"Get back," Tuthmoses yelled at the elephant, waving his arms.

Everything obeyed the pharaoh.

Everything, that is, except frightened elephants. It smashed through what remained of the wall. It turned to run along the path, and its madly swinging trunk struck Tuthmoses, knocking him over. In running past, its back leg landed squarely on Pharaoh's chest. The elephant stampeded on, smashing everything in its path, but nobody noticed.

Pharaoh lay in the mud. Blood welled up from his chest and soaked the ground where he lay. His breathing made awful bubbling sounds.

Djus ran to the pharaoh and, with tears running down his face, knelt in the mud at his side. He reached out to lift him from the mud, but when he saw the extent of his injuries, he grabbed his hand instead.

The world had changed. The rain beat down unnoticed. All stood immobile, staring.

When Djus finally stood up and faced the crowd, everyone in the circle fell to their knees. "Pharaoh, Pharaoh," they murmured.

Djus set his shoulders straight and shook his head. His eyes met Susan's over the backs of the people.

"Bring the Hery Seshesta," he ordered. "Akheperenre is dead."

A servant jumped up and hurried to obey.

Then the wailing began.

CHAPTER 31

WHAT NOW?

Susan stood, stunned. Djus bowed his head over Pharaoh's body, and the rain beat down on them all.

Susan wasn't sure what she should do. She wanted to move beside Djus, to be a friend to him as he was to her, but he looked so withdrawn she didn't want to intrude.

A low, slow drum beat began, and as Susan listened, it grew louder, and she heard a deep voice singing. Through the driving rain, an apparition trod slowly toward the spot where they all stood. Susan saw a man—the legs and body of a man. The head rose high—an animal head. The head looked from side to side, searching.

It looks sort of like a dog. Susan shuffled back a few paces to let the thing pass.

"Anubis. Anubis." Susan heard the whisper from the people around her. "Hery Seshesta," she also heard.

A line of white-clad men accompanied the Hery Seshesta. Their singing, so low and sad, exactly expressed how Susan felt. Akheperenre had been her friend. She had felt safe in his presence. She thought of him laughing and joking; or glittering with gold; or dozing in the sun. With his death, her world had changed. Every life in Egypt had changed.

Susan walked forward and gently pulled Djus away from the body so that the Hery Seshesta and his attendants could begin their work. They picked up the body and gently laid it in a large wooden box they brought with them.

The priests shut the lid on the box, and the sound of it closing seemed to close the episode. People began to move again. Harsheer spoke quietly to the Hery Seshesta as the attendants lifted the coffin and left with them as they carried the box away.

"Pawara. What happened to Pawara?" Djus asked, looking around.

Susan gulped. *How could we forget about him?*

Off to the side, they saw a small knot of people gathered around a woman kneeling in the mud. She wailed and pulled at her hair.

Djus and Susan hurried over.

Pawara lay on his back in the mud. Blood bubbled from the deep wound in his chest. His body was broken. The woman wailed.

Djus fell to his knees in the bloody mud. He took Pawara's hand in his.

Pawara's eyes flickered open. His lips moved. Susan could see that he was trying to speak, but no words came.

Djus understood the question, though. "Pharaoh has moved on to the Field of Reeds," he said, bowing his head.

Pawara closed his eyes. With a sigh, his last breath left his body. He, too, was dead.

And the wailing continued.

Djus rose to his feet. He shuddered from head to foot. Then he squared his shoulders and addressed the people standing around.

"I am Useramen," he said. "I am the son of the grand vizier of Egypt, the Right Hand of Pharaoh."

People murmured and shuffled their feet.

"Your governor, Pawara, is dead. May he live on in the Field of Reeds."

The people just looked. They said nothing. They did nothing.

"Right," Djus said. "We need another Hery Seshesta for Pawara. I need a troop of soldiers with chariots to speed the news to Thebes. Go to the palace and ensure that everyone and everything is safe from this rain."

Susan could see the relief on people's faces as they hurried to obey. *They needed someone to take charge,* she realized.

As the people hurried away to tend to the tasks they'd been given, Susan watched Djus. He stood tall and straight, quietly and calmly giving orders and solving the problems that were brought to him. The rain beat down, and so they moved from the smashed menagerie into a drier area of the palace.

All that terrible night, Djus stood like a pillar holding everything together.

As dawn broke over the river, the rain stopped, and the sun broke through the clouds. A tall man strode into the presence of Useramen. Dressed as a warrior, he removed his helmet and scratched at his grizzled head as he came forward. He bowed deeply.

"I am General Merimose," he said.

Djus visibly slumped. "Where were you?" he demanded.

"On patrol to the south," Merimose answered. "There's been a bit of trouble with one of the tribes, and Pawara didn't want any unpleasantness while Akheperenre was visiting."

"Hmph," was all the reply Djus made.

General Merimose looked around at the wrecked hall. Boxes and bundles were heaped on tables and beds. The floor had a slick of mud covering the mosaics. The place looked terrible. "You have done wonderfully well, in awful circumstances, Your Excellency," he said, bowing deeply again. "You will make a fine vizier."

"Hmph," Djus said again. "Not for a long time yet."

Djus stood up straighter and struck a gong. The sound reverberated through the palace corridors. Servants, soldiers, and even the cooks rushed into the room to answer the summoning.

"I, Useramen, son of the grand vizier of Egypt, tell you now that I have appointed General Merimose as the temporary governor of this place. Let it be so."

Djus bowed to the general and the general bowed deeply back. The people stood still and silent.

Susan came up beside Djus, and as the two of them turned and left the room, they could hear Merimose ordering the people to their tasks.

CHAPTER 32
MAKING A MUMMY

Susan led Djus back to the boat. He was exhausted—so was she.

Teo and Hori stood by the gangway and pushed mugs of hot milk into their hands as they clambered aboard. Djus sat huddled in on himself, and Susan sat quietly at his side. She hoped that it would be enough that she was there, because there wasn't anything she could say to make the situation better.

Later in the day, having slept more deeply than she expected to, Susan wandered down to the water butt. Djus was already there, sitting quietly, staring back at the second boat, which Harsheer and the embalmers had taken over to begin the funerary rites for Akheperenre. Susan sat, too, drinking from the cup in her hand. Hori and Teo were also sitting quietly. The four of them formed a small circle of quiet inaction.

The only sound Susan could hear was the steady drone of the priests' chanting. Susan could see where they were working. A sail had been stretched along the length of the boat so that they worked in the shade. She could see the box that had carried the body to the boat, but now it was set to one side and a large table was set up under the sail.

As they all watched dispiritedly, a priest came to the side of the boat and drew water from the river. He carried the bucket under the awning, and then they heard a splash and saw water running out onto the deck. The water ran red.

"What are they doing over there?" Susan wanted to know.

It was Hori who answered. "I went often with the magician Harsheer to stand guard over the rites," he began. "First they wash the body in the waters of the Nile. Then they make a puncture here." Hori pointed to a position just above his hip on the left hand side of his body. Susan shuddered to think of this happening to her good friend just there on the next boat. "They remove all the important organs," Hori continued.

"Like what?" Teo asked.

Djus drew a shuddering breath.

Hori continued. "They take the intestines, the stomach, the lungs, and the liver. Each is preserved separately and kept in a separate jar."

Djus looked up. "Is that all they remove?"

"Ah." Hori nodded. "The brain, sir. They remove the brain."

Susan had to know. "But how…"

Hori shrugged. "They get it," he said.

Djus sighed and swiped at the tears running down his cheeks. "You've gone this far. Tell us the rest," he said.

Hori inclined his head in agreement. He wriggled into a more comfortable position and leaned forward. "They have wire hooks," he said. "They poke the hooks up the nostrils and wriggle it around"— he showed them with his fingers—"and gradually bit by bit they pull out the brain."

Susan rubbed at her nose; suddenly it felt itchy.

"But who was the Hery Sh…Hery?" Susan couldn't remember what they had called the person in the mask.

"The Hery Seshesta," Djus and Hori said together.

Susan nodded. "What does he do?"

"Well, he is the chief embalmer," Hori went on. "He wears the mask of Anubis who is the god that presides over the judgment of the dead."

"So, Anubis is like…a dog?"

187

"No, Anubis is the jackal god," Hori supplied. "In the desert the jackal is the animal that scavenges the dead."

"The heart," Susan said, shuddering. "What happens to the heart?"

"Ah." Hori nodded knowingly. "That stays because Anubis will weigh that against Ma'at's feather to judge the worth of the person."

"But, Hori, what else happens to the body? It's not a mummy yet." It was Teo who asked the question.

Hori continued with the story. He told how the body would be rubbed with precious oils and continually washed. "The cleansing takes fifteen days," he said.

Djus stirred. "Can they do the cleansing while we travel on the river?"

Hori nodded. "I should think so."

"Then we have only fifteen days to get back to Thebes," Djus decided.

They all nodded, but nobody moved.

Hori continued. He told them how after the cleansing, the body was packed inside and out with natron, which was a type of salt found in the desert. This would dry the body out.

Then, he said, they would pack the body cavity with linen and fragrant herbs to give it more of the fullness of life. Finally the body would be wrapped in linen bandages. Round and round the body with amulets and jewelry hidden within the linen strips.

"Do they have enough linen strips with them?" Susan worried.

Hori smiled and shook his head. "Seventy days it takes to prepare the pharaoh for his tomb. We will be in Thebes long before there's a need for linen bandages."

While they had been sitting, listening to Hori, the sun had dipped below the horizon. They noticed a slight chill in the air. As one, they stood, stretched, and moved toward the smell of food cooking. A meal had been prepared and was laid out in the stern of the vessel. They picked at it a little, drank only water, and quietly moved to their bed rolls for more sleep.

Susan lay on her palette, hearing the chanting priests, thinking of all that was happening on the other boat, missing her dear friend who was now just a body.

Akheperenre is still out there somewhere—I can feel it. And then Susan slept.

CHAPTER 33
ENEMIES

At first light the next morning, they left the ruined palace and began the slow journey back to Thebes. The news traveled faster along the shore, and people lined the banks, crying and wailing as the boats passed.

Flowers draped the boats, and everywhere they stopped along the river, people rushed to the shore with more flowers to add to the garlands.

Djus was the highest-ranking official in the flotilla. As he was the son of the grand vizier, people looked to him for direction. He was expected to deal with even the smallest details of the awful trip along the Nile to Thebes.

Susan could see that he was worried. Something was not right.

She found him one day, sitting on a coil of rope, staring out at the river as it carried them northward.

Susan wasn't sure how to begin, but she sat close to him on another coil of rope and waited.

"Egypt is in great danger," Djus said quietly. "Our great country will soon be thrown into turmoil. Our enemies will gather."

"Why are you so sure that will happen?" Susan moved closer and put her hand on his arm.

"Our pharaoh-to-be is two years old. Who will lead? Many will want to, but who can command our armies? Who can make the sacrifices to keep our land safe?" Djus sighed. "I can hear the rasp of our enemies sharpening their weapons in the soughing wind."

Djus fell silent and stared out at the river.

"But your father is the grand vizier. You are doing such a good job of organizing this trip. Your father will continue to order the country until Tuthmoses comes of age." Susan tried to sound hopeful.

Djus shook his head. "We will try," he said. "We will work hard to keep Egypt strong. It is our duty." He stood and turned directly to Susan. He shrugged. "We are not of the royal line." He said it as though that fact explained the whole problem.

Then Djus strode down the deck to talk to the captain of the boat.

Susan looked after him and then turned her attention to the following boat and the awful burden it carried. She missed Akheperenre so much.

CHAPTER 34

HEART

Susan stood in her favorite spot in the front of the boat. She was physically exhausted but not sleepy. Harsheer was off with the embalmers, and Teo and Hori were sitting together, quietly talking.

She never knew what made her think of it, but all of a sudden, the thought was there, fully formed and dreadful. Akheperenre was dead. He would be sealed in his tomb. There hadn't been time. Her crystal wasn't grown yet. The tomb would be sealed.

Susan's legs gave out, and she slumped to the deck. She sat there, staring at nothing. *I want to go home. Oh, crystal, I need you. I miss you. I want to go home.* Round and round the words circulated in her head until she was dizzy. Tears slid down her cheeks and dripped onto her knees.

At the first opportunity, she questioned Harsheer about the sealing of the tomb and the crystals.

"I'm busy," he said, pushing her away. "I've got important matters to tend to."

"You brought me here. Now you have to make it right so I can go home," Susan demanded.

Harsheer shrugged. He actually shrugged. Susan couldn't believe he could be so callous.

"What will I do if I'm stuck here? What will my parents do?" Susan grabbed his arm.

He pushed her off. "I'm busy. Don't you see? I was Akheperenre's priest and magician. Who will be the new pharaoh's priest, and how can I make sure that I still have a court position?"

Susan cast around for an argument that might work on this selfish man. "But…But you went to a huge amount of trouble to drag me here. Are you just going to give up on all that?"

Harsheer shrugged. "There'll be other magics," he said. "I've been interested in a theory about ways to turn copper into silver—I'll work on that."

Susan glared. Harsheer sidled up to her and whispered confidentially. "Do you think that Useramen and his father would be interested in a way to turn copper into silver?"

Susan shrugged, turned on her heel, and marched away.

Her home, her family, her hope, all swept away by a frightened elephant. Susan sank onto her knees in the bow of the boat and stared sightlessly ahead.

Susan had no idea how long she sat sunk in despair, but the next thing she noticed was a gentle rasping sound. It stole into her consciousness, a steady rasping sound that went on and on. The sound got inside her head and niggled at her.

She jumped to her feet, determined to put a stop to the irritation. *Ow.* She staggered. She had been kneeling too long. She stamped feeling back into her legs. The gentle rasping continued.

The boat was tied to the shore for the night, and someone—probably Teo—had wrapped her cloak around her shoulders. The only other sound was the gentle lapping of water against the side of the boat. The rasping, scraping sound continued. It felt like sandpaper on her skin.

Susan marched down the length of the boat, seeking the source of the irritation, and found Djus squatting against the side of the boat. Two little oil lamps lit the area in front of him, and he was so intent on what he was doing that he was totally unaware of Susan's approach.

Her heart caught in her throat. Susan felt guilty for being so absorbed in her own problems and upsets that she had forgotten how Djus must be feeling. She approached him quietly.

Djus gasped in a quick breath. "Susan, you startled me."

Susan bowed her head. "Vizier," she said.

Djus smiled. "Please don't say that. It's bad enough without you saying that. You are my sister in friendship—stay that…. Please? When we're alone, be my friend."

Susan sighed a deep breath. "OK," she whispered. She wanted to put her arm around him but thought he might shy away, so she hitched forward to see what he was doing.

His hands held a stone. It was a little smaller than his fist, and it looked as though he was trying to shape it with a larger stone and a copper file.

Djus saw what she was looking at and held up the stone. "I wanted Akheperenre's heart stone to be made with love," he explained. When he saw her blank look, he explained. "The embalmers had to remove the heart from his body. It was crushed by the elephant. But they need to have a heart there so they will place a stone heart in place of the real one."

Susan gulped. *Gross.* She sat back on her heels. What could she say? It seemed so strange to her. But…this was their land, and this was her friend. What else mattered really?

"Djus," she said softly, "isn't green stone supposed to be sacred and magic?"

Djus nodded and sniffed a little. He looked up at her with a question in his eyes.

"Wait here," Susan said and hurried off to the spot where her chests were stored.

It only took her a moment to find her green stone, and she hurried back to Djus with it. It felt so right to give it for Akheperenre's heart stone.

Djus's eyes lit when he saw it. "That is a stone of great magic. Where did you get it?"

Susan explained how she had landed on the stone. She skirted the story of why she had been drawn here and what was happening in the pharaoh's tomb, but as she talked, she took the copper file and began expertly shaping the stone into a heart. Susan became so absorbed in the task that she didn't notice Djus staring at her fingers.

"You have great carving skill, Susan," he said.

So then Susan told him all about her mother and how she carved great blocks of stone and of the different things she made. As she talked about her mother and her home, her voice grew wistful.

"You are indeed far from home." Djus patted her arm.

The two sat in companionable silence. By the time the sun rose over the river cliffs, Susan had the stone shaped to their satisfaction.

"I'll take it to the priests," Djus said, standing up.

"No, we're not finished yet. We have to polish it."

Susan stood, too, and pushed Djus into the river. "We need river sand for the polishing," she said and jumped in after him.

Djus rose to the surface, blowing and gasping for air. He pushed Susan under as she came to the surface, and soon the two were rolling and playing in the water.

Refreshed, Susan dived deep and returned to the surface with a handful of sand. Djus caught on and he dived, too. Teo, coming to the side to see what the splashing was about, brought them a pot and leaned over the side so they could fill it with the sand.

That day, as they progressed down the river, Djus and Susan took turns using the fine, wet sand to polish the stone heart.

"Now we rub it with oil," Susan ordered. And they did.

It burnished to a beautiful, satiny sheen.

Djus pulled his knife from his belt and carefully scratched something into the surface. Susan leaned forward to see. "What does that say?" she asked.

"It says 'a good man,'" Djus replied.

"That's a lovely thing, Djus," Susan said gently.

Hardly daring to hope, she put out her fingers. "May I write something, too?"

Djus looked at her in surprise. "Can you write?"

"No, not in Egyptian, but I can write in my language."

Djus handed over the stone. Susan turned it to the other side and carefully scratched two words into the green surface.

Susan handed the stone back to Djus and watched as he ran his fingers gently over her letters.

"What do these markings say?" he asked

"'My friend,'" said Susan.

Susan watched Djus's eyes fill with tears and felt her own tears spill out onto her cheeks.

"Let's take it to the priests." She sniffed, jumping to her feet.

Djus rose to join her, and together, they launched his little reed skiff. They climbed in, and Djus cast off the rope. They bobbed on the river for only a few moments before the other boat overtook them. The boat where the embalmers were working to purify the body of the ex-pharaoh of Egypt. Akheperenre. Her friend.

The embalmer-priests bowed low to Djus, and to Susan's surprise, they bowed to her as well.

"Daughter of Ma'at," the Hery Seshesta intoned. "It is fitting that you bring us the heart of the pharaoh to be judged by Ma'at's feather in the afterlife."

Susan bowed back.

The priests hurried the pair back into their skiff, and Susan and Djus had to stroke madly to catch up with their own boat. It took them quite a while and some vigorous exercise to make it back into the shade of the larger boat. Djus threw his line to the deck, and the two clambered aboard.

Susan found she was exhausted from her sleepless night and the sudden exertion. She slumped gratefully onto her cushions and wriggled in for a good sleep.

The curtains whisked aside, and Djus stood in the gap. "I'm going to teach you to write properly," he said with a grin.

"OK," she mumbled sleepily and drifted off into the most refreshing sleep she had had in a long time.

Djus was as good as his word, and for the rest of that terrible journey down the river, the two of them studied Egyptian reading and writing. They used slivers of stone and scratched the symbols with a harder piece of stone or used a burned stick to mark the stone. Djus was surprised at how quickly Susan learned the basics. Soon she was able to read the inscriptions on the temples they visited. It filled the hours and helped them forget about Akheperenre with the embalmers in the following boat—for a little while.

CHAPTER 35

THEBES

Everyone, it seemed, had crowded onto the riverbank to watch the funeral boats arrive in Thebes. The boats flowed past the first temple and soon were abreast of the city. A low murmur came from the crowd. It carried across the water to the boats, like sadness made solid.

Susan stood at the side of the boat, staring at the shore. Harsheer had insisted that Susan be fully dressed as a princess, and Teo had spent an hour painting her face and decking her in all her finery. Harsheer was dressed in fresh priestly robes as well and stood next to her. It seemed to Susan that there were thousands of people crowding the riverbank.

The river seems to have gone down. I guess the flooding is over. Susan shook herself; it didn't feel right to notice such unimportant things at such a time.

When their boat turned toward the shore, the boat carrying the body of Akheperenre and the embalmers turned farther into the current and headed for the western shore.

Susan strained to see where it was going.

Harsheer leaned close. "They are taking the body to the Wabet across the river. To prepare Akheperenre for being sealed in his tomb," he explained with a smirk.

Susan turned her back on him and stared off into the distance.

As their boat neared the shore, a trumpet blast drew all eyes to their boat. Djus stood in the bow. Tall and proud, he was wearing his grandest clothing. He looked very much the son of the grand vizier.

We all have a part to play here.

Susan sighed and moved to stand beside him.

As she turned from Harsheer, he grabbed her arm and bent to whisper in her ear. "Remember you are my daughter. I adopted you. You have friends here, and you must use your position to make us rich."

Susan wrenched her arm away and hurried along the deck to where Djus stood. She wanted to rub her arm to get rid of the feel of Harsheer on her skin. *It's started already, just like Djus said it would,* she thought ruefully.

They heard an answering trumpet blast from the riverbank, and Hatshepsut came into view. An honor guard of soldiers stood at attention, making a path for her. She was dressed as brilliantly as she had been for the Opet Festival, and she glittered in the sun as she walked sedately to the shore. At her left side walked Neferure. She, too, glittered from head to foot. Her beautifully pleated skirt swished as she walked, showing glimpses of her blue leather sandals set with lapis lazuli.

On Hatshepsut's right side, holding tightly to her hand, toddled the next pharaoh. He, too, glittered in the sunlight. Perched on his head was a small version of the double crown of Upper and Lower Egypt. Tied to his chin was a small false beard. He scratched at the gold dust on his chest.

Their boat bumped gently on the stone steps, and all on board bowed low.

"Your new pharaoh greets you," Hatshepsut called in a voice that carried over the crowd. "Your new pharaoh welcomes you home at this sad time."

A hush fell on the assembled people, and all strained forward to hear every word.

Djus clasped his hands tightly behind his back and inclined his head to Hatshepsut. "Mother/Aunt of Pharaoh." He bent his head slightly to Neferure. "Sister of Pharaoh," he said gravely, "I thank you for your welcome. I am greatly saddened by the circumstances."

Then Djus bowed very low to Tuthmoses standing next to Hatshepsut. "Pharaoh, live long," he said.

"May your reign be fruitful and to the greater glory of Egypt."

The toddler pharaoh just stared until Hatshepsut nudged him with her elbow. He looked up at her, and she motioned with her hand. He turned to Djus and made the same gesture.

Hatshepsut turned, and she and Neferure, with the two-year-old pharaoh in tow, moved sedately back through the honor guard and into the palace.

Other nobles and court officials who had been on the dock to greet the vessel jostled and pushed into a straggly line behind them. Susan saw Harsheer push himself in between two other priests near the head of the line.

Djus stepped off the boat when he saw his father, Amehtu-Ahmose, at the top of the ramp. They greeted each other with bows, then stood, grinned, and hugged. They strode away, talking busily together. There was a lot to plan. Susan found herself left behind.

The honor guard dispersed, and Susan straggled up the riverbank alone.

By the time she reached the top of the bank, the nobles, officials, and Djus and his father had disappeared into the palace. Susan sighed and looked back over the river.

The Nile spread out before her, stretching as far as she could see to right and left. Farther downriver she saw the boat carrying Akheperenre's body to the embalming place—the Wabet, Harsheer called it. She shuddered to think what the embalmer-priests would be doing to it. *Seventy days to perform all the rites and prepare the mummy for burial in its tomb.*

"Two months I've been here," Susan whispered. "Fifteen days on the river, that leaves fifty-five days more to prepare the mummy and then just a few more days to seal the tomb. That's not quite five months I will have been here and the tomb will be sealed forever." Susan strained her eyes westward. She knew her crystal was growing in its rocky niche in the sacred tomb on the other side of the river. Growing—but not fast enough.

A tear slid down her cheek and dripped onto her chest. Another followed it while Susan stood still, waiting for the tears to go away.

It was almost dark when she finally turned and headed into the palace to find her way to her rooms.

CHAPTER 36

BREAKFAST WITH USERAMEN

Susan saw little of Djus over the next few days. Sometimes she saw him in the distance, hurrying along with his father, deep in conversation. Once when he hurried by quite close to her, Susan saw that he frowned and looked uncomfortable. Susan sighed; he looked unhappy.

Susan spent her time wandering the palace, watching everything. She felt like an outsider. Everyone was busy, they had no time for her. Teo went to the kitchens to bring her meals on a tray. There were no banquets that she was invited to. The palace didn't feel like a home to her. When she had had Djus's company, she had felt comfortable around the palace, but now he was busy and she was no one. She had no task to occupy her time. She was Little Princess Stranger.

The only place Susan felt at all at home was in the local temple of Ma'at. The priestesses made her welcome there. Often she would sit in the courtyard and watch the worshippers bringing their offerings to the goddess. Many of the people who came looked sad; some cried openly.

The priestesses explained to her that they were bringing offerings so that the goddess would help judge their loved ones kindly. Egyptians believed that when a person died, the goddess Ma'at used her feather so that Anubis could weigh their soul—they called it Ka—on his scales. The Ka sat on one side of the balance, and the ostrich feather from Ma'at's head went on the other. A good person's soul would balance against the feather, and the person would pass into the Field of Reeds to live in eternal happiness and splendor.

⇒⊹ ⊹⇐

Eighteen days after their return to Thebes, a soldier brought Susan an invitation from Useramen—still Djus to her. The invitation arrived early in the morning. The sun was barely over the horizon, and the palace was just stirring.

Susan grabbed a fresh sheath and knotted a belt around her waist as she hurried to the door. She carried her cup of warmed, honey-sweetened milk with her.

"Wait, Princess, you can't appear before the grand vizier's son dressed like that." Teo hurried after her and caught her arm. "He is an important official of the court now, and you must be dressed like a princess to enter his presence."

Susan thought about it for only a moment. "He is my friend," she said. "I should be able to appear before him any way I want. And also," she added, "I haven't seen him in ages. He's invited me now, not an hour from now when I'm all dressed up."

Susan skipped out the door and hurried along the corridor after the soldier.

Djus sat on a big pillow, nibbling apricots from a plate set on the small table before him. As soon as Susan entered the rooms his face lit up in a big smile. He waved her over to the table and pushed a little plate toward her.

Susan was relieved to see that Djus was casually dressed, too. A simple kilt—nothing more. He wasn't important right now—he was Djus. She plopped down on a pillow next to him and grinned. "Hi," she said and relaxed.

Over breakfast Djus and Susan chatted quietly together. They had a lot of catching up to do. Susan hadn't been busy, but Djus had, and he filled her in on all the things that had been happening to him over the last days. It sounded to Susan as though he'd been living in the center of a whirlwind.

Finally, Djus drew a deep breath and placed his goblet carefully on the table. "Susan," he said and then hesitated. He looked down at his hands, then looked up at her again. "Princess Merit-Amen," he began again, more formally. Susan was surprised at the formality and raised her eyebrows. Djus looked at her for a moment before continuing. "It is expected that my father will be named as the regent and ruler of Egypt at Tuthmoses's kingship ceremony tomorrow. I will be expected to take up a position at his side. I will have a lot more to do. My friends are already asking for favors from me."

Susan nodded. She nibbled a green leaf from the platter on the table.

"You have asked for nothing. You were my stalwart friend when we brought Akheperenre back to Thebes. I would reward you. Whatever is in my power," he blurted out, waving his arm in an expansive gesture.

Susan looked at him in surprise. "Are you sure?" She fiddled with her cup on the table. *The thing I want is time, time for my crystal to grow and form.* She looked down at her fingers around the cup.

"There must be something," Djus urged.

Susan looked up at him. "Be my friend," she said. "Always be my friend." She grabbed his arm and looked hard in his eyes. "One day, there may be a way for me to return home. Then I will need your help." She shook her head—sad. "Always be my friend."

Djus laughed. "That is too easy," he said. "Harsheer will not be happy that you haven't asked for a higher position for him," Djus warned.

Susan tossed her head. "I'm not happy with Harsheer," she said. Then she stopped; her head quirked to one side. "You know, Djus," she said, "I've just realized that I've seen Hatshepsut and Harsheer together a lot since we've been back. Do their duties mean that they have to work together?"

Djus shrugged. "Not particularly." Djus jumped to his feet and a frown pulled his brows together. "I keep forgetting I'm Useramen, son of the grand vizier. I can't dismiss such things anymore. Maybe they're plotting." Djus began pacing the room. He looked worried.

Susan rose, too. "Try not to worry. I'm your friend. I'll watch them."

Djus stopped pacing and sighed. "Thanks, Susan, it will make me feel better having you with me. At least one person I trust to be my friend, someone who doesn't see a means to power when they look at me."

"What about Nebka and Dauuf?"

Djus shrugged again. "They see me as a stepping stone to my father. Dauuf has already asked to be made governor of the Delta of Lower Egypt, and Nebka asked me to appoint his father head of the army." Djus shook his head sadly.

Susan laid her hand on his shoulder. "All this stuff is still new. You'll get used to it in time."

Djus patted her hand. "It's a very dangerous time for Egypt. A toddler for a pharaoh—many kings outside our borders see us as weak."

"But Egypt is not weak," Susan assured him.

"Huh," Djus retorted. "You haven't heard about all the noble families in Egypt who think this is the ideal time for their family to become the Great Ones." Djus shook his head. "There are plots within plots."

"I'll watch." That was all Susan could think of to say.

Djus sighed. "You have helped already. Having a trusted ear for me to talk to has helped me prepare for tomorrow." He sighed again. "But now I must go. I have to meet my father to go over plans for tomorrow's ceremony."

Djus pulled a flower from the vase on the table and handed it to Susan. It was a lily. She smiled and gave him a hug. He seemed so beset.

"Huh," he said. "I almost forgot. I have a place for you at the ceremony tomorrow."

"Me?"

"Yes, I want you standing with my father and me. You are a princess and my friend. It will give you status in court outside of Harsheer's influence."

This was a huge honor, and Susan wasn't sure whether to agree or not. "Are you sure you want me to do it?"

Djus nodded. "Absolutely."

Susan nodded, too. "I'm going to be really nervous. I won't know what to do." Djus laughed. "You'll be fine. You just have to stand there and look princessly."

Susan sighed. "I'll try not to trip over the cushions," she said.

They both laughed, and Djus hurried away to take up his duties.

Susan strode off back to her rooms. She felt more relaxed. *I have a friend. I am a princess after all. Egypt is a good place to be. I have a home here.*

Her steps slowed, and her heart sank. *I have a home here* echoed in her head. She felt as though she was betraying her mum and dad and her whole life before Egypt.

Susan felt torn in two. She wanted to go home. Her life here was pretty good and looked as though it would get even more interesting, but her mother and father…Susan tried, but she couldn't summon pictures of them in her head anymore. Susan walked to the riverbank and stared across the Nile to the opposite shore, where her crystal grew in the tomb. Too slowly. Too slowly. And her life in Egypt wrapped around her in the sights and smells and sounds of Thebes. She turned back to the palace with a sigh.

CHAPTER 37
HARSHEER

It took hours for Teo to prepare Susan for the naming ceremony. Djus sent Lady Miew to help as well.

First the bathing, then the anointing with oils. They carefully wove beads and gems through her youth lock. *It's grown really long.* Susan was surprised to see that her youth lock now reached down to her shoulders. Susan sighed. *Time, time again. I've been here about three inches of hair growth.*

The face painting seemed to be one of the most important parts of the preparations, and the two ladies bent over Susan's face as though it were an art project.

Teo, with her tongue sticking out between her lips, carefully drew an eyebrow, starting at Susan's nose and carefully sweeping out toward her temp…

Bang.

The door burst open. Teo jumped and shrieked and drew the eyebrow up onto Susan's head.

Harsheer stood in the doorway. He was fuming.

"What is going on here?" he demanded.

Susan sprang to her feet. "Out," she said, pointing to the doorway.

Harsheer swaggered into the room. "You are my daughter." He smirked and folded his arms across his chest. "I demand to know what you are doing."

Miew stepped forward and bowed low. "We are preparing Princess Merit-Amen for the naming of the king," she said.

Harsheer waved his hand dismissively. "There'll be none of that," he said. "I don't need you to be there."

Susan glared at him. "First you want me to be influential; then you don't. Make up your mind."

"I don't need you there, daughter," Harsheer sneered. "Now wipe that mess off your face, and go swim in the river or something."

With that, Harsheer turned on his heel and marched out of the room.

Susan slammed the door behind him.

The three stood. Susan, Teo, and Lady Miew. Silence made a nice barrier after the yelling and banging.

Miew took Susan by the shoulders and gently pushed her back onto the stool. She wet a sponge and began to remove the eyebrow streak that Teo had made. "You are lucky that Teo didn't paint your eye," she said.

Teo squeaked, but Susan laughed. "Djus wants me at the ceremony. I will be at the ceremony," she said.

CHAPTER 38

NAMING PHARAOH

The main hall of the palace was festooned with garlands of flowers for the occasion. On a dais at one end of the hall stood the imposing seat that the new pharaoh would occupy.

We should get him a booster seat for it, Susan thought as she stood next to Djus.

Susan had plenty of time to look around. They had been waiting for about an hour. It was hot in the room and getting hotter as the day wore on. Susan smoothed down the pleats in her skirt. The pendant of Ma'at felt heavy on her chest. She loved to run her fingers over the texture, the smoothness of the glass, and enamel against the ridges of Ma'at's wings. It was one of her most prized possessions.

Djus explained to her that his father was off preparing Tuthmoses and that he would parade him in
to the sound of trumpets. The priests would crown
the little king and declare Djus's father the regent.
Then the toddler could go have his nap, and they
could all go to the feast. And Egypt would go on as
always, with Djus's father making all the decisions in
the pharaoh's name until he was old enough to rule
for himself.

Susan looked around. She didn't see Harsheer
anywhere in the crowd. She wanted him to see that
she was in attendance and looking every inch a princess. But he wasn't there. And what was holding up
the ceremony?

The curtains behind the throne opened a little,
and Djus's father slipped through. His face was a
mask. No expression whatsoever. He took his place
to the left of the throne.

Susan and Djus exchanged glances. This wasn't
what they were expecting.

The trumpets blared. The curtains swept aside.
There was Hatshepsut, standing regally at the top
of the stairs. She was lavishly dressed and glittered
with gold dust. She swept into the room and seated
herself on the throne.

It was only then that Susan noticed Tuthmoses
following along in her wake. A soldier brought a

smaller chair, which was placed next to Hatshepsut, and Harsheer lifted the toddler onto it.

Silence. In that great hall full of people, there was silence.

Hatshepsut wriggled into the cushions, making herself more comfortable.

She plans to be there for a very long time, Susan thought.

Harsheer scanned the crowd. His eyes skimmed over Susan. She saw a flash of annoyance cross his face, but his eyes swept on.

Harsheer took a deep breath and announced, "Hear you, all gathered here. Queen Hatshepsut, great wife of Pharaoh Akheperenre, daughter of Pharaoh Aakheperkara, has graciously consented to act as regent to our blessed Pharaoh Tuthmoses III."

There were murmurings in the crowd. People looked at one another. Some were surprised, and others smiled as though they were in on the secret.

Harsheer rapped his staff on the floor. "Greet your new pharaoh," he ordered. "His throne name is Menkheperenre."

"Menkheperenre," the crowd murmured as they bowed deeply.

Hatshepsut stood. She lifted Menkheperenre from his smaller chair and, holding his hand firmly, began a slow parade across the hall. The crowd parted before them.

Hatshepsut, we can see. The little pharaoh is down around people's knees. Susan stood on tiptoe to spot the little guy.

"Menkheperenre," the crowd kept repeating. Hatshepsut walked regally on, keeping the little pharaoh at her side.

Harsheer followed close behind. As he drew level with where Susan stood, he used his staff to crack her on the shins. He walked on.

Djus's father, Ahmose, followed along behind Harsheer. Djus fell into place beside him. Susan hurried to join him in the slow progress across the hall and out onto the balcony.

The people of Thebes were assembled below. They had come to see their new pharaoh. To them, this was a splendid sight. They cheered and waved. Hatshepsut inclined her head haughtily, and Menkheperenre lifted his little hand to wave. Djus's father stepped forward and lifted the child into his arms so that the crowd could see him and he could see the crowd. Menkheperenre waved harder. The crowd cheered.

Annoyed, Hatshepsut waved her arms to the soldiers standing by, and they, in turn, opened the beer and wine casks that were set up for the celebration.

The crowd quickly moved over to the tables piled with food and drink.

CHAPTER 39

POLITICS

The day dragged on. Hatshepsut sat on the throne in the Great Hall. She glittered. Stiff, erect, queenly in every movement she made, she held little Menkheperenre on her lap.

All the nobles, the important officials, and the priests came forward one by one to offer congratulations to the new pharaoh and to lay gifts at his feet.

Looks more like they're laying gifts at Hatshepsut's feet to me. Seems like she is the one getting the congratulations. Susan watched.

Harsheer stood at Hatshepsut's elbow, looking smug and self-satisfied. Susan carefully used her left foot to gently rub the sore spot on her right shin where Harsheer had cracked her with his staff.

Menkheperenre quickly became restless and started wriggling to get down. Hatshepsut waved an

imperious hand, and Neferure hurried out from behind a curtain and took the little pharaoh away. *She
does not look happy*, Susan noticed.

Oh, Neferure will be expected to marry him, Susan
remembered. For the first time—ever—Susan felt
sorry for Neferure. *She'll be waiting.*

The afternoon dragged on. The line of important people offering congratulations and gifts continued. It was even more obvious with the little
pharaoh gone that the nobles looked to Hatshepsut
to further their ambitions.

Finally, Hatshepsut stood. The audience was
over. Everyone in the hall bowed deeply to her. And
while all heads were bowed, she slipped through the
curtains behind the throne and was gone. So was
Harsheer.

Djus's father jerked his head at Djus, indicating that
he should follow him as he left. Djus grabbed Susan's
hand, and they quickly left the Great Hall together.

⚔

"What happened?" Djus wanted to know.

Djus and Susan were alone with Djus's father,
Ahmose. They sat on cushions in a quiet corner of
the garden. The pool at their feet was very still in the
late-afternoon sun. Only frogs could be heard in the
garden. In the distance Susan could hear the townspeople celebrating their new pharaoh—loudly.

Menkheperenre, meanwhile, was having his afternoon nap.

Taking a deep breath, Ahmose began to explain.

"When I arrived at the child's rooms to fetch him to the throne, Hatshepsut was already there and had the boy well in hand. She was dressed in full queenly style. Harsheer was there as well, intoning prayers to every god he could think of." Ahmose paused to sip his mint tea.

"But Egypt needs strong leadership. Our enemies are laughing," Djus interrupted.

Ahmose shook his head. "I don't think so. You saw the Hittite ambassadors making offerings like all the other envoys. Would you fight Hatshepsut?"

"Well, no," Djus conceded.

"What makes our neighbors rich is trading with a peaceful Egypt. Throwing their armies at our towns costs them money. I looked at the situation, there in Menkheperenre's rooms. There is more danger of unrest within Egypt than from without," Ahmose continued.

"But," Djus protested.

Ahmose held up his hand and shook his head, smiling. "Hatshepsut is the daughter of one pharaoh and the great wife of another. During the reign of Akheperenre, she was often the person making the decisions and giving the orders. People didn't see that side of her, but she is an able administrator. She is also the stepmother of Menkheperenre, our current pharaoh."

Ahmose paused to sip his tea. Djus and Susan exchanged glances but said nothing.

"Unity at the top is what will keep all of Egypt strong. Internal strife over who will be regent would probably result in no regent and some ambitious upstart as pharaoh. I only had a moment to decide, but this is the best way forward for Egypt."

Ahmose smiled and bowed from the waist. "After all," he said, "I am still the grand vizier. The Nile still flows."

The three sat on their cushions in the quiet, sipping their tea as the sun sank below the cliffs on the west side of the Nile.

CHAPTER 40

ENTOMBED

All too soon the fateful day arrived. The day when the mummy of Akheperenre would take his last journey up the winding path to the hidden Valley of the Kings. To be placed in his tomb and the entrance sealed forever. Susan sighed. What could she do? Harsheer and she had begun the crystals only four and a half months ago. She counted them off: *Paopi, Athyr, Khokiak, Tybi.* The crystals were only two-thirds grown. Susan tried to imagine what her crystal would look like if it were only two-thirds full size. She held her fingers up, but it was no use.

A trumpet blared. Time to assemble. Susan hurried through the palace corridors. They were so familiar to her now. She pushed through the crowd, which parted and bowed to her, and slipped into place among the priestesses of Ma'at.

Susan wore a long sheath of the finest linen. The pleats were knife edged. Over it she wore a long cape. Painted around the hem were creatures and birds, set among flowers and reed beds. It swirled as she walked, making the creatures appear to move as though they were alive. Susan loved the way the cape made her feel, and she loved the effect it had on the people who watched.

"She is a magician," she heard whispered.

"She is Ma'at's Chosen," was the whispered reply.

"She was honored by Akheperenre," she heard some say.

Susan smiled and touched the symbol of Ma'at that always hung around her neck. The chief priestess smiled, too, and reached over and gently set an ostrich feather into Susan's youth lock.

Hatshepsut stood motionless at the head of the line. She glittered with gold dust. Neferure and the little pharaoh stood behind her.

Menkheperenre's cloak fell in one straight line from his shoulders to the ground. The attached amulets and brooches made it so stiff that he looked like a little statue. The twin crowns of Upper and Lower Egypt perched on his head. The red and the white. In his hands he clasped the crook and the flail, the two most powerful symbols of the Egyptian pharaoh.

He looks uncomfortable and unhappy, Susan observed. *So does Neferure.*

Next in line stood the grand vizier, Ahmose, and Djus stood stiff and proud at his side.

The next in the parade were the priestesses of Ma'at. Susan maneuvered so that she was directly behind Djus. She put her foot forward and gently kicked his heel. Djus started and turned quickly. His scowl turned to a smile when he saw who had touched his foot. Susan winked. Djus winked and turned front again.

His shoulders look more relaxed now, Susan observed.

Then Hatshepsut waved an imperious hand. Trumpets blared, and the procession started out of the palace grounds toward the River Nile.

The mummy of Akheperenre already lay on his special boat. It was enclosed in an elaborate case that was painted with symbols of the gods and with a face that looked something like the man had in life.

There's no twinkle in his eye, though. Susan looked hard but just could not equate this stiff thing with the friend she had known.

The boat was decorated with flowers and fruits and vegetables. Incense burned in several pots around the mummy case. A couple of oxen stood tethered to the stern. They added their frightened lowing to the cries and screams of the official mourners. These women loudly lamented the pharaoh's passing and pulled at their hair and clothing. Hatshepsut, the wife of Akheperenre, stood rigid with her face expressionless.

She's the one who should be mourning the most, Susan thought.

Other boats pulled into the shore and took on all the people from the procession. Susan climbed onto the second boat with the priestesses, and it headed out across the river, following Akheperenre to his final resting place.

On the west bank, priests took up the burden of the mummy and began to trudge up the worn pathway to the tomb.

Harsheer joined the parade, too. He preceded the mummy and the mourners, making gestures and mumbling incantations.

It's a lot farther now than it was before, Susan saw as she trudged along in the dust and heat. *The river was a lot higher last time I came here.*

Several times along the way, the party paused to drink, and at each stop, a different group of priests took up the burden of the pharaoh. The crying and screaming and the persistent beat of the drums made Susan's temper ragged long before they reached the rim of the valley. Menkheperenre found the whole experience way too much for him. First he whimpered, and then he wailed. He hit out at people with his little flail. Finally he refused to budge. He stood screaming and sobbing. His tears had washed streaks through the gold dust on his face. Neferure grabbed his hand and tried to pull him along. She tugged; Menkheperenre howled louder. She stamped her foot; Menkheperenre kicked her.

Ahmose bent forward and picked up the little pharaoh. The parade moved forward again.

Hatshepsut was now farther ahead because she had neither paused nor paid any attention to Menkheperenre's upset.

Ahmose soothed the little pharaoh, and he soon put his baby head down on the shoulder of his grand vizier and fell asleep.

Thankfully the official mourners stopped at the rim, and only a handful of people accompanied the mummy into the Great Place. The sudden silence sounded loud in Susan's ears. Only the wind sighed through the cliffs.

Harsheer led them down toward the tomb. His hand gestures became more emphatic, and then his hands were glowing and small explosions occurred along the side of their path. "Demons, demons," he cried. *Bang.* "Demons, demons." *Bang.*

I guess he needs to prove that he is of some use as a magician, Susan thought.

The doors to the tomb gaped wide open, and a servant stood to the side, bowing deeply. Right in the entrance, the parade halted. The case was opened, exposing the mummy of Akheperenre inside. Priests clustered around and began chanting. Each held an amulet in his hands, and each brought the amulet to where the mouth of the mummy would be. They also touched where eyes would be.

"They're making sure that Akheperenre will still be able to hear and see and speak," Djus whispered to her. "They call the ceremony the Opening of the Mouth."

Susan nodded to him as she watched the priests close and reseal the mummy case.

Each person took a torch from the stack by the door and lit it as they entered the tomb.

The passageway was so narrow that they could only walk two abreast. Djus lit two torches and walked slowly beside his father and the sleeping pharaoh. The mummy followed. It was eerie in the semidark, and the flickering torches made the figures in the pictures on the walls seem as though they moved just out of view. The parade descended a long flight of stairs and then passed along another long, straight passageway.

Susan remembered the trap in the floor and faltered to a stop, peering ahead into the darkness.

"It's covered for now," Harsheer whispered in her ear. "Move on. Nobody is supposed to know you've ever been in here, remember?" Harsheer pushed her in the back, and Susan stumbled forward again.

After another flight of stairs, they entered a large room. The walls were painted with bright pictures of Akheperenre's life. When Susan had hurried through the room on her visit with Harsheer, there had only been two torches, and so she had not noticed the beautiful paintings on the walls. The room was now stacked with every kind of household furniture and item that Akheperenre might ever want to use. Susan noticed small models as well. She recognized a model of a bakery with little clay people working at the tables and thrusting tiny loaves into a circular oven. Other models showed ladies weaving fine cloth.

"Akheperenre must want for nothing in his afterlife," Djus whispered in her ear. He bent beside her, and they admired the little figures together. "He will still be powerful in his life in the Field of Reeds." Djus reached out a finger and stroked the clay figure of a cat.

The passageway to the next chamber led out of the room on the left and Susan and Djus hurried along to catch up with the rest of the party.

The main room that held the sarcophagus was enormous. Susan hadn't realized just how large it was on her first visit. Two large painted pillars held up the ceiling.

The ceremony of lifting Akheperenre into his sarcophagus took quite a time. Priests chanted and sang, and Susan could tell that they were giving the pharaoh instructions on how to proceed from here to pass through the tests and trials that would allow him to arrive in the Field of Reeds, which seemed to be a sort of heaven. Hatshepsut stood at the head of the sarcophagus, and Susan drifted back through the crowd until she was leaning against the wall.

Susan let her mind drift, searching for her crystal. Could she sense it growing in its little niche? She thought of the four crystals growing there—so close—and began drifting quietly along the wall toward their hiding place. Using her hand, she felt behind herself for the slight indentation that would tell her where they were.

I just want to check on them, she told herself as she sidled along the wall. Her hand scraped on the indentation, and she turned quickly and squatted low to have a closer look. She brought her torch down very close to the spot. Yes, she could see the outline of the niche. The picture Harsheer had magicked to hide the hole wasn't perfect.

Susan reached for her little knife, hardly daring to breathe.

A hand grasped her wrist. "Can you sense it, you stupid girl?" Harsheer sneered in her ear. "If you can't sense the crystals, then they aren't ready."

Susan fell back against the wall. "I have to see," she whispered.

Harsheer looked over his shoulder. Everyone still listened to the priests chanting to speed the pharaoh on his way to the Field of Reeds. "Little fool. Open it now, and the four will be destroyed forever. There'll be no chance of you ever getting home then." Susan could smell the onions on his breath as he pushed his face into hers.

"Once the tomb is sealed, there's no chance of me getting home anyway." Susan waved her hand in front of her face and screwed up her nose.

"I don't know why you even care, Princess, best friend of the grand vizier's son. Why would you want to leave?"

Susan struggled out of his grasp and pulled herself up to her full height. She glared up at him. "Yes, I have friends here," she said. "What about you? Do you think the regent, Hatshepsut, is your friend? Huh!" she sneered.

And with that Susan slipped quietly back into the crowd around the sarcophagus.

Susan helped the priestesses with the rest of the ceremony. She even helped to lower the lid of the sarcophagus into place. No matter what her hands did, though, her attention was on a tiny niche hidden in the wall. There, her crystal and three others grew quietly—she hoped.

Sadly, even with all her attention focused on the one spot, she felt nothing from her crystal. Nothing.

When everyone left the tomb and the huge doors swung closed for the last time, Susan felt as though she was cut from her home. The Internet, movies, cars, planes, television, slammed behind a door and gone from her forever.

She walked beside Djus out of the valley. What else could she do?

CHAPTER 41

EXILE?

Two days after the closing of the tomb, Susan was summoned to the main audience hall. The soldier who escorted her was a stranger to Susan. He was stiff and polite, but unfriendly. A scar ran down one side of his face, and he walked with a limp.

It looks as though he has been injured in battle, Susan decided. *This soldier is a warrior.*

The audience hall was a large area where the main business of Egypt was undertaken. Even at this early hour, scribes sat about, busily scratching on slivers of stone or, if the record was to be more permanent, painting on papyrus sheets.

Soldiers lined the walls. *This is new.* They were drawn up formally and stood rigidly at attention.

Each carried a sword on his hip and a spear in his hand. Shields were propped against their legs.

Susan hesitated at the top of the stairs. *This is way more formal than usual.* She looked around to see if she could see any sign of trouble. Everything seemed peaceful but not comfortable. *Things have changed almost overnight.* She walked quietly down the steps and stood beside the seated scribes. They glanced quickly at her but then bent their heads to their work again. She was curious to know why she had been summoned. Susan settled in to wait and watch.

Between the soldiers, the audience hall was bustling. Officials hurried in and out through the archway, and small groups stood about in the courtyard beyond, chatting and swapping gossip. Attendants moved among them, offering drinks and fruit on silver trays.

A trumpet blast caused every head to turn to the doorway. Hatshepsut moved into the room, swaying and nodding haughtily to right and left. Harsheer walked just behind her, peering around her shoulder and looking pleased with himself.

Seating herself on the throne-like chair at one end of the hall, she surveyed the room with a look of great satisfaction. Most of the people had fallen to their knees, in obeisance to her. Susan stood straight and bowed her head to Hatshepsut.

Officials hurried forward to present their concerns to the queen. *The regent,* Susan reminded herself. With a flick of her hand, Hatshepsut caused them to backpedal and stand to one side.

"Where's that mud princess?" Hatshepsut used her loudest voice.

Uh-oh. Susan stepped forward and bowed again. She didn't speak. Others shuffled away from her so she stood alone before the throne.

"Ah, yes." Hatshepsut looked down her nose. "You do not belong in my palace," she said. "You were once welcome here, but things have changed." Hatshepsut pointed to the door. "Leave," she said.

Susan fell back a pace in surprise. She glanced quickly at Harsheer. Had he planned this?

Harsheer did not look pleased. He stumbled forward. "Oh, Great Queen"—he bowed very low—"I thought you were going to ban her from your presence." He bowed even lower. "I know that my adopted daughter can be a great trial to the princess Neferure—and to you." He rushed on. "But she is dear to me. She is of my household. I need her here in Thebes with me."

Well, that's news to me, thought Susan.

Harsheer grabbed her arm and pulled her forward. "Bow low, you little fool," he whispered in her ear. Susan bowed.

"Hmph," muttered Hatshepsut. "I don't see any use to her. Get her out of my sight and keep her away from Neferure and the pharaoh Menkheperenre." She waved her hand in dismissal. Harsheer backed out of the hall, bowing all the way. He pulled Susan along with him. She tripped and stumbled. Being pulled backward made her clumsy. So embarrassing.

"Her manners are deplorable," Susan heard Hatshepsut say as she reached the stairs and hurried from the room.

In the courtyard Harsheer turned on her. "Can't you ever do anything right?" he demanded.

Susan pulled her arm from his grasp. "I didn't do anything. You looked pretty smug when you entered. What did you think was going to happen?"

Harsheer harrumphed and rubbed his foot over the mosaic on the floor. "It doesn't matter now. Just keep out of her way. That's all. And stay away from Neferure, too."

"Happily," Susan retorted. "Why don't you send me back to your estate with Teo if I'm so much trouble?"

Harsheer looked up through his lashes. "Erm," he faltered. "I do need you here in Thebes with me."

"Don't see why."

"Well, there might be some other magic to do," he said with a shrug.

"Yeah, right." Susan turned on her heel and stormed off.

I wonder why he wants me here, she wondered. *There's something else in his selfish mind. I'm sure of it.*

CHAPTER 42

THE CRYSTAL OF
THE NORTH

Life in the palace settled into a routine. Everyone rose early to take full advantage of the cool morning air. Susan dressed quickly and usually met Djus for breakfast. He was kept busy with official duties now, and so this was often the only time they could spend together.

The river had settled back into its banks, leaving acres of gooey black mud. The farmers toiled in the fields. First clearing the paddocks and then restoring the system of water canals. As soon as all was in place, they could plant the crops for the year. As the land dried out, beasts were used to draw water from the river and splash it into the canals so that the farmers could water their plants.

The land drowsed in the heat.

But this was a busy time for Djus. As the son of the grand vizier, he always had something that needed doing or some emergency that needed special attention. Often Susan helped him out. She had nothing better to do and found that drifting around idly, as a princess, got boring very quickly.

Because Djus had taught her to read the Egyptian hieroglyphics and to write in the Egyptian hand on the boat, she sometimes acted as a scribe. She found that she liked copying out reports. She learned a lot about how a nation runs. She saw that Hatshepsut was fully in charge now and that Egypt was at peace and still prosperous.

Harsheer rarely spoke to her, but she often saw him scowling at her from the corners where he whispered with other priests and, more and more often, with Hatshepsut.

Susan still occupied the same set of rooms in the palace, and Teo still acted as her maid.

Thankfully, Teo wasn't crying and sobbing much anymore. It seemed that her friendship with Hori had blossomed into love, and Teo now seemed much happier with her life in Egypt.

Susan sat bolt upright in bed.

Crystal! She could feel her crystal. It was like the tug of an old friend.

Laughing, she held out her hand, hopeful that her crystal would appear on her palm.

Nothing. Susan sighed.

She grabbed her sheath from last night and dashed through the palace. She needed to be as close as she could to her crystal, the Crystal of the North. It tugged her on.

Her feet led her to the riverside. Looking west, across the wide stretch of the Nile, she could feel her crystal calling to her. She held out her hand again, hoping against hope that her crystal would come to her. It didn't.

She turned back into the palace. Her steps dragged as she walked back to her rooms.

All day, as she went about her daily routines, her thoughts were across the river, deep in the tomb with her crystal. She didn't hear people speak to her. She left most of the food on her plate at meals. Teo found her in the afternoon sitting by a reflective pool, staring at nothing.

"Princess, I've looked everywhere for you. What is troubling you?"

Susan jerked out of her thoughts. "Nothing, Teo. Everything is fine," Susan said.

Teo looked doubtful. "Come, it is the heat of the day." She tugged at Susan's arm.

"OK." Susan sighed and stood.

"Magician Harsheer asked after you today. He is worried that you may be becoming distracted," Teo said as they walked along.

Susan looked at her quickly. "Really? Why would he care?"

Teo smiled. "Oh, Princess, he cares a great deal. Every day he asks me how you are doing. He notices how you are dressed and what you eat. He is always asking me questions about you. He comes with clothes and jewelry for you."

"He's been spying on me!" Susan yelled. "He's been using you to spy on me."

Teo began to wail. "No, no. He cares. He said so."

"And you believe what Harsheer says?"

Teo gulped.

Susan grabbed Teo's hand and hurried her along to their rooms. There she sat her down. Susan took a deep breath to calm herself, and then she explained to Teo that Harsheer was not her friend. That he was spying on her and using Teo to find out things that he knew Susan would never tell him.

"He's been using you, Teo." Susan shook her head.

Teo sobbed quietly. "Hori told me that Harsheer was mean, selfish, and ambitious. But Magician Harsheer seemed nice the way he told me he cared about you."

"Hori is right." Susan nodded. "You and Hori are really good friends now, aren't you?"

Teo smiled through her tears. "Yes, Princess, we will one day start our own family and have our own house and farm. We dream of that day."

Susan smiled, too. "Well, I wish you luck with that. It will be good for you two to get away from that magician."

Susan lay on her bed, but she didn't sleep. The constant pull from the Crystal of the North kept her feelings on edge. And now she had another problem. Harsheer was spying on her. *That's why he wanted me to stay in the palace*, she realized. *He still wants to use me to get at the crystals.*

When it was time to rise for the evening, Susan had a plan.

CHAPTER 43

THE PARTY

"Teo, tonight I want you to dress me in something new. Some of those clothes and jewelry you told me Harsheer brought to me."

"Really, Princess?"

"Yes, Teo. He spied on us. Now we are going to trick him. We are going to be so normal and boring that he will be just wasting his time."

"But—" Teo began

"Doesn't matter what is really going on, Teo," Susan interrupted. "We will tell him what we want him to believe and then do whatever we want underneath."

"But..."

"You can do it, Teo. You'll see. And," Susan added, "we start tonight."

"How?"

"Hmmm, send down to the kitchens. We are going to hold a dinner party tonight." Susan began pacing the room, waving her arms around as her plan unfolded. "We haven't ever used the eating room of this suit. Tonight we will. And…We'll invite Djus and Dauuf and Nebka to come and ask them to bring friends. I think we'll need some musicians, too."

Susan sat on a cushion and pulled her scribe desk onto her lap. She wet her ink cake and pulled out her favorite brush.

"We'll send Hori with the invitations to the group."

"But why?" Teo flicked her fingers in worry.

"Why?" Susan laughed. "So that when Harsheer asks you how I am, you can tell him all about the party and how happy I am. And how there's no need to worry about me. That I'm settling in to palace life very well."

"Huh." Teo hurried off to make arrangements in the kitchen.

⇒⋅⇐

The evening was a great success. Everyone had a good time. They all laughed again at the episode where Djus and Susan had won the swimming race against Neferure.

But even though Susan laughed and chatted with her guests, her background thoughts and feelings were across the Nile in the pharaoh's tomb where her crystal called to her.

I'm coming. I'm coming, she thought. *I don't know how, but I am coming.*

CHAPTER 44

THE PULL

Everything that Susan did from then on was to the background of the tug of the crystal. She could feel it calling to her in every thought, every task. Her crystal was pulling at her from across the Nile and through Pharaoh's tomb.

Every waking moment, she could feel the pull. The crystal was insinuating itself into her dreams as well, so that she woke in the night yearning for her crystal.

But—and it was a very big but for Susan. Her crystal—all four crystals—were sealed in Akheperenre's tomb. He had been kind to her, and she understood that he was in his resting place, and she didn't want to disturb that rest. And there were guards and the river and a desert and a tomb. Her crystal was so out of her reach. But it still called to her.

Susan worried around and around the problem. Sitting by the reflective pool in the cool of the evening, she saw a glint in the water and for a nano second she thought it was her crystal shimmering there.

One evening, eating dinner with Djus and his family, she knocked the food from his hand because it looked to her, for a moment, as though he was about to swallow the Crystal of the North.

She apologized profusely to Djus and to his family, but she thought they were looking at her in an odd way. *You're getting weird Susan*, she came to realize.

One day she came to herself standing on the riverbank staring across the water. She had no idea how she had arrived there. She had no memory of walking out of the palace, or walking through the streets. There were tears flowing down her cheeks. All she could feel was the pull of her crystal.

Wiping her face on the hem of her shift, Susan squared her shoulders. *I can't go on like this,* she thought. *Next thing I know I'll be trying to swim across the Nile.* She cocked her head to one side. *Hmm, it looks over a kilometer across and look at that current.* She shook her head. *I don't think so.*

She planted her feet more firmly and put her fists on her hips. *Whatever it takes, I will have to rescue the crystals from the tomb and go home. They have to be out in the world so that they can maintain balance. The world needs those crystals. I need my crystal.* Susan nodded her head with determination and turned toward the palace. *I have some planning to do.*

Even with the decision made, Susan found it a difficult choice. On one hand, she missed her home, her parents, her friends; on the other hand, if she left, she would miss, Djus, Teo, and her life in Egypt. *It will be like losing Jeremy all over again*, she thought. But her crystal still pulled. She went often to the riverbank, peering across to the red cliffs that hid the Valley of the Kings from view.

Standing on the riverbank one day, Susan felt a brush on her arm, and when she started away, she saw that Harsheer had joined her. He peered down at her. "Six months are up, daughter," he sneered. "The crystals are probably grown and just sitting there, all locked up where you can't get them." He smirked.

Susan waved her hand airily. "Crystals?" she lied. "I haven't thought about them in ages." Then she added, "Do you still wonder about them?"

Harsheer looked out across the water and nodded slightly. "Yes, I do."

"Well, I guess you failed again." Susan shrugged. "And, anyway," she added, "they're way beyond anyone's reach to even check on them."

Harsheer said nothing but continued to gaze across the river.

"Well, I guess you've got a daughter for all time." Susan turned on her heel to leave. "Oh"—she turned back briefly—"thanks for the new clothes and the jewelry. Nice."

She walked back into the palace with a great show of being casual about it.

I've got to get out of here.

CHAPTER 45

THE PLAN

Susan turned all her thoughts toward leaving. As soon as she began to seriously plan what it would take to leave Egypt, the pull of her crystal became less insistent. It was as though it could sense that she was coming for it.

Susan looked around her rooms. It had all become so familiar to her. The river scene painted on the wall, the look-face, the chests holding her clothes. And even more important the friends. Djus, his father Ahmose, the other boys, and Teo. *Teo has become more a friend than a servant,* Susan realized.

And the experiences! What experiences I've had. Susan smiled at the thought. She had landed on a rock that was now the heart stone of Akheperenre. She had received a falcon feather that first morning—she still had that. Then she had sneaked the little statue that Harsheer used to pull her to Egypt. She was keeping a close watch on that. And then she had slipped out of Harsheer's rooms with the scroll of Ma'at.

And there she stopped. *Oh, I'm not keeping that. I know where that has to go.*

—◈ ◈—

Susan called Teo to her. "We're going out," she said. "I need a bag to carry some stuff in."

Soon, Susan was ready to leave.

Into the bag she stuffed the scroll of Ma'at. Susan picked up the collar of Ma'at to put in the bag as well, but she paused, caressing the wings that spread along Ma'at's arms. Susan sighed. "I'll wear this," she said. *One last time.*

—◈ ◈—

"Ma'at's Chosen, you are always welcome here." The priestess, Takaret, smiled and ushered Susan in through the large wooden doors. "Share mint tea with me," the priestess offered. "It is too long since your last visit."

They sat on plump cushions and sipped quietly at their tea. Susan didn't know how to begin. She looked up from her tea and saw that Takaret was smiling at her. She smiled back.

"I've brought you some things," Susan said and pulled the bag onto her lap.

The priestess put her hand over Susan's and shook her head gently. "Let's talk first," she said.

"Ma'at, in her wisdom," Takaret began, "saw that you were the perfect person to share in the creation of her crystals. She could see that your goodness and caring would be a strong buffer against the greed and self-interest of Harsheer."

Susan blushed. Takaret hurried on.

"He had the skills and talent to make them but not the wisdom and grace to use them wisely."

Susan nodded. She could agree with that.

"Akheperenre's sudden death caused you great difficulty and distress, we know," continued the priestess.

Susan hung her head.

"You have behaved with courage and dignity. We have seen that you are a very resourceful person."

Susan looked up. "My crystal is calling to me," she blurted out. "I can feel it all the time."

Takaret nodded and smiled. "As I was saying," she continued, "you are one of the most resourceful people I have ever met."

"But the crystal is trapped in Akheperenre's tomb. His resting place. It's calling and calling, but how can I disturb his rest? I'll feel like a tomb robber." A tear slid from Susan's eye and tracked along her cheek. She sipped at her mint tea.

"We here at the temple of Ma'at knew Akheperenre quite well. He was a just and fair man. His kingship sat lightly on his shoulders. We know that he had great affection and understanding of your plight. He often called you by your given name, Susan, when in my presence."

Susan looked up sharply. "He knew where I came from? He knew my name?"

The priestess nodded and smiled. "None of us fully know where you were born, but we all know it was far away and unreachable from here. He will understand," she said.

For a moment Susan felt a surge of hope. Then she sighed. She had to get across the river and into the valley. Harsheer was watching her still. She had to break into the tomb. Find the crystals. And…And…She had to sneak away and leave all her friends without saying good-bye or anything. Her shoulders slumped.

"Harsheer is watching me. He knows that the crystals should be grown by now. How can I get across the river without him seeing me?"

"Ah, in two days Hatshepsut and a lot of the nobles will be going across the river to the dedication of Akheperenre's mortuary temple. It is now complete. Join that group and go over to the dedication."

Susan slowly shook her head. "That won't work unfortunately. I have been banned from the presence of Hatshepsut, Neferure, and Menkheperenre."

"Really!" Takaret laughed. "Really, she did that. We hadn't heard." The priestess shook her head. "She always was bossy." She slapped down her teacup and poured herself some more mint tea. "I think we can help there," she said, pouring more into Susan's cup as well. "You will be part of our official dedication group. You will be a representative of Ma'at at the ceremony."

Susan felt hopeful. "You can make that happen?"

"Ma'at can make that happen," Takaret retorted.

Susan felt as though a great weight had lifted from her shoulders. "I came to return these things," she said. Susan opened the bag and pulled out the scroll of Ma'at. She handed it to the priestess, who held it reverently in her two hands.

Takaret's face softened. "Thank you, Susan. You have returned a great treasure to our temple. Thank you."

Susan smiled shyly. "I took it from his table and hid it," she said. "I didn't want him making any more magics out of it."

Takaret nodded with a smile. "Very wise."

Susan bent forward and the weight of the collar of Ma'at shifted on her chest. "Oh," she said, "I must also return this."

Takaret held up her hand. "No, no, Susan. That was especially fashioned for you. It is yours. Wherever you are. Whenever you are, you will always have that reminder that you are Ma'at's Chosen."

Susan stroked the collar. "Thank you," was all she could say.

The priestess rose and pulled Susan to her feet. "Go well, Susan, and return early on the morning of the ceremony."

They walked to the door together.

The heat was a blow after the shade of the temple, but Teo waited there, in the shade with an ostrich plume fan, and they set off back to the palace.

CHAPTER 46

THE PREPARATION

The next two days passed in a blur for Susan. All the places and all the people—she would be leaving them all behind. She took the time to visit some of her favorite places within the palace. The garden courtyard where they would sit in the cool of the evening, the riverbank where they would go to swim as a group. Susan was very conscious that everything she did was for the last time. She was sad but also excited at the thought of holding her crystal in her hand again.

Susan found there were some things that she just couldn't leave behind, and so she began packing herself a small bag. Her gold necklet was the first thing in the bag. How could she leave that honor? Her falcon feather. The little statue that Harsheer had used to bring her to Egypt. These were her things.

And now she thought of home. For so long she had pushed thoughts of home and family away, but now she could begin to think of arriving home again. Her mother, her father, her bedroom, Judy.

There was danger ahead, and she knew it. Entering Pharaoh's tomb was punishable by death— if you were caught. Death, and not an easy one either. Susan tried not to picture herself lying on the desert floor with spears sticking out of her chest. And then she remembered the traps set within the tomb itself.

She gasped. Best not to forget the traps. She squared her shoulders. Her crystal tugged at her very being. *I'm coming. I'm coming.*

Then the day arrived. Susan rose as soon as the first tinge of pink lightened the sky. Teo helped her into her most beautiful sheath and then painted her face carefully. Blue around her eyes to bring out their color, black painted eyebrows. She settled a wig over her head—it was specially woven to fit over her youth lock. Next Teo draped her beautiful, soft woolen cape around her shoulders. Lastly she clasped the collar of Ma'at over the cape.

"You look beautiful, Princess." Teo stepped back and sighed. "You are a princess, you know," she added.

Susan looked at Teo. She had grown up. Susan thought of the crying, wailing girl that she had first encountered. Now Teo was confident and sure of herself in her surroundings. Susan took a step forward to give her a farewell hug. She stopped herself. The less Teo knew of her plans, the safer she would be. When she disappeared, Susan needed Teo to be as surprised and puzzled as everyone else. *Hori will look after her,* she thought.

Hori. And Teo. Susan smiled. She reached into her bag and pulled out her honor necklet. Quickly she undid the catch and removed a quarter of the golden beads.

"Here, Teo," she said. "I want you to take these. I don't want you to wait and save any longer. I want you and Hori to start on your family and your life together as soon as possible." Susan thrust the beads into Teo's hands.

Teo looked up at her with hope shining in her eyes. "But who will look after you?" she wanted to know.

"Um…Miew will help," she said quickly. "Don't you worry about that, Teo. Keep the beads with you, but not on show. I want you to have a wonderful life."

Teo bowed low. "Oh, Princess, you honor me. I hope you will come visit our home once we are settled. We would be so honored."

Susan bowed low, too. "Thank you, Teo. And thank you for all your help." Susan straightened. "Well, enough of this," she said. "We must hurry to join the priestesses on the riverbank."

The boat waited. Festooned with flowers and painted in bright colors, the boat shone in the early-morning light. People gathered on the riverbank, standing around in small groups chatting and laughing.

Susan slipped in among the priestesses who were standing to one side, quietly watching the proceedings. Takaret caught Susan's eye and nodded and smiled. She held out a plume to Susan, who quickly slipped it into her wig. All the priestesses of Ma'at wore the plume as a symbol of Ma'at.

Susan noticed Teo. She was standing on tiptoe, whispering in Hori's ear. Susan could tell from their smiles what they were talking about.

And there stood Harsheer. He did not look happy to see her. He scowled and fidgeted, he could do nothing to oust her from among the priestesses. Harsheer wasn't that powerful.

A burst of laughter drew Susan's attention to another group of nobles who were standing close to the water's edge. Djus stood with his father. He nodded and smiled to her as she caught his eye.

How different this group is to the last time we gathered here, Susan thought. *Then we were taking Akheperenre to his tomb. All the wailing and the hair pulling.* Susan shook her head at the memory.

Djus had explained to her that the dedication of the mortuary temple was a celebration of Akheperenre's life. He was a god now, and the mortuary temple was built so that people could visit him, make offerings, and speak with him. It was a place for quiet reflection and peace.

I will enjoy celebrating his life, Susan thought. *He was always good to me. I miss him.* Then she gulped, thinking of her plans for his tomb. She involuntarily held out her hand, willing her crystal to appear, but her hand remained empty. "I'm coming. I'm coming," she whispered.

A trumpet fanfare blared through the morning quiet. All attention turned to the palace doorway. Hatshepsut stood there. *Glittering as usual,* Susan noticed.

Hatshepsut made her stately way down the walkway to the boat. All bowed their heads as she passed. Susan bowed hers particularly low so that she would not be noticed among the priestesses. Her plume bobbed on her head, but she kept her head low.

Neferure followed closely behind her mother. She was looking down her nose and mincing along, nodding to right and to left, but somehow she could not match the haughtiness of her mother. Especially as she was dragging Menkheperenre along beside her. He was sucking his thumb.

Adorable. Susan grinned.

The royal three proceeded up the gangplank onto the boat, and all the other celebrants hurried after them. The drumbeat sounded out across the water, and the boat drew away from the riverbank. The sun rose behind them and cast the shadow of the boat before them as they rowed for the western bank, the mortuary temple—and, for Susan—Pharaoh's tomb.

CHAPTER 47

THE CELEBRATION

The mortuary temple stood on the river plain just on the edge of the cultivated land. The party moved through the green of the newly growing fields and into the sandy yellow of the rock. The temple was a simple structure, made of stone. Dominating the eastern wall of the temple was a larger-than-life statue of Akheperenre, and in front of that was a stone table where people could place their offerings of food and drink for him in his afterlife.

The day was filled with singing and dancing. Food was spread on tables as well as offered to Akheperenre. Everyone ate and drank their fill. Susan maintained a low profile and kept well away from Hatshepsut, Neferure, and Harsheer. The priestesses of Ma'at surrounded her, and she moved within their group.

By midafternoon the ceremonies drew to a close. People sat chatting quietly or had already moved away to return to the riverbank for the trip back across the river.

Takaret summoned Susan to her side, and when she arrived, she was surprised to see that Djus and his father, Ahmose, were also standing with the priestess.

"We will be leaving soon," the priestess announced. "But we need some reliable people to remain here and see that everything is tidy and in good order." She rested her hand on Susan's shoulder. "I have designated the princess Merit-Amen to stay and have instructed her servant to pitch her tent among the palm trees."

Ahmose then announced with a smile, "I have decided that my son, Useramen, will also remain, to ensure that all is well here. I must return with Hatshepsut and Menkheperenre to Thebes." He turned to leave.

Harsheer blocked his way. "What?" he yelled. "You're leaving these two in charge here."

Ahmose looked down his nose at Harsheer. "She is your daughter—you say. I have found Merit-Amen to be a responsible person, and she and my son work well together, so that is what I decree."

"I'm staying, too." Harsheer pulled at his beaded collar. He made a couple of hand gestures and mumbled some weird words, but as nobody seemed scared by the gestures, he stalked away.

Not so magical without the scroll of Ma'at, are you, Harsheer? Susan thought with satisfaction.

Soon the temple region became quiet. Harsheer had grumbled off to have his camp made ready under the palms. The last stragglers hurried through the fields to the river's edge, eager to return to Thebes.

Susan supervised the sweeping of the courtyard and set others to clear away the remains of the feast. She ensured that the incense pots were all smoking properly.

Then she went searching for Djus.

Susan found him standing before the statue of Akheperenre. As she stepped into the shaded niche from the heat of late afternoon, Susan could feel the peace seep into her tired bones.

Slipping her sandals off, she let her toes spread on the still-warm flagstones as she padded over to a bench placed to the side.

Djus had not moved or in any way signaled that he knew of her presence, but Susan was sure that he was aware of her. Djus was like that. He always knew everything that was going on. *He will make a great grand vizier,* she thought as she sank gratefully to the bench.

The statue's pose was rigid and showed Akheperenre staring off into the west. *At least he's sitting down*, Susan thought. In life he had always looked so relaxed, draped lazily along a bench or on a pile of cushions on the floor. Now he looked stiff and kingly. There was nothing of the Akheperenre she knew in the statue in front of them.

As though he had heard her thoughts, Djus whispered, "Do you think he's here?"

Susan waited before she answered. The smoke from an incense pot drifted lazily around the statue's knees. The air was very still. The light reaching into the niche through the portico of the temple bathed the statue in a golden glow.

"No, I don't think he's here, Djus."

Susan stood and came forward. Reaching as high as she could, she draped the garland of flowers she carried over the statue's lap. The whiff of lotus and papyrus flowers was strong in the air, even stronger than the myrrh of the incense.

"You're right, Susan," was all Djus said. He turned on his heel and walked out of the temple.

Susan hurried to catch up and almost banged into his back. Djus was transfixed in the courtyard, looking up.

Susan looked up and gasped. The sky was afire.

The golden ball of the sun was hanging on the ridge of the cliff. It looked huge. Great fiery streaks radiated out from the sun, turning the whole sky shades of red, orange, and gold. As they watched, it seemed the sun poured its essence into the top of the cliff.

"Ah." Djus sighed. "The father Amen-Re has come for Akheperenre."

Susan nodded.

"The sky is red, as they celebrate their joining together. It is a great omen, Susan."

Behind them in the temple, Ramose, the temple priest, had begun his chant as he made offerings to the new god Akheperenre. The high, singsong voice was oddly comforting as it reverberated against the cliff face before them. The dust under their feet was still hot and giving off a smell of burned sand.

The two stood shoulder to shoulder, unmoving, as the sun finally sank behind the cliff. The red glory gradually faded to a soft purple and then a nighttime blue. Suddenly Susan shivered. There was a chill in the air now. She rubbed her bare arms.

Djus started to attention. He turned and smiled at her. "He is truly with the gods in the Field of Reeds now. I know it."

"It was a glorious sunset," Susan agreed.

"We've kept everyone waiting long enough, I think." Djus smiled.

They ran down the hill together, bare feet leaving puffs of dust in their wake. *Thank goodness I took my wig off earlier,* Susan thought as she flicked her sidelock back behind her shoulder. Her necklace of Ma'at bounced on her shoulders with every step she took.

Djus was ahead of her and moved to the seats set around a fire pit. Susan slowed her pace and walked more sedately the last few paces. Hori and Teo were tending the fire and watching the sizzling skewers of duck meat, which smelled wonderful in the still evening air.

Susan watched them laughing together, nudging each other and joking in the firelight. She settled next to Djus and stretched her hands toward the warmth. So peaceful a scene. Susan sighed, thinking of what she must do when all were asleep.

CHAPTER 48

THE EXECUTION

Susan held her breath as she slipped quietly out of the tent into the balmy Egyptian night. So far from the river, the air felt dry and crisp as she crept quietly toward the edge of camp. Holding her bag close, she leaned carefully against the trunk of a palm and looked around in the starlight.

At home the stars are never so bright, she thought as she peered around the trunk, looking for the sentry.

And then she spotted him, Hori stood with his back to another palm. Both hands clasped his spear in front of him, and his head drooped forward onto his hands. Susan slipped quietly around behind him to the water skins.

She knew she needed to take water with her. Most of the skins were empty, waiting to be filled in the morning, but she pushed several aside until she felt the damp squishiness of a full skin. She carefully pulled it from the pile. It squeaked against the other skins, and Susan froze in place. What if someone heard?

Only the sound of the palm leaves clicking in the soft breeze came to her straining ears. She pulled again on the water skin until it came free in her hands. The sigh of relief turned to a gasp when someone grasped her wrist in a cruel, angry grip.

"What are you doing?" Harsheer whispered in her ear.

"I…I was thirsty," Susan stammered in reply, holding up the water skin.

"Where's Teo?"

"She's asleep, and I didn't want to wake her."

"Humph," Harsheer grunted, "I'll escort you back to your tent, Merit-Amen, and there will be no more straying around the camp at night."

Susan bit her lip and allowed herself to be taken back to her sleeping place. She pulled back the curtains and entered without a word. Now she had to wait to be sure Harsheer had gone to his own tent and to sleep. She settled on her pallet, sitting up, clutching the water skin. *If I lie down, I'll fall asleep myself,* she knew. *This is my only chance to get the crystal.*

Susan waited in the dark until she was sure hours had crawled by, and then gathering the water skin and pulling her cloak about her, she once again slipped from the tent.

Hori was still leaning against the same palm trunk, and Susan crept quietly through the sleeping camp and out into the desert.

She hurried along the pathway, glad the starlight was bright enough to travel by. Stones cut her feet and the grit caught in her sandal straps, but her feet were a lot harder now than the first time she had been carried along this path. Susan hurried on.

The path quickly led up into the cliffs, and Susan was glad of all the swimming and walking she had been doing in Egypt. It was a hard climb, but she was making good time, it seemed.

She was surprised at how quickly she arrived at the guard house, which barred the way into the valley. She could see an oil lamp burning in the window and moved a little off the path to creep around behind the little building. The path here was steep, and she had to go down the cliff a little and scoot along sideways to get around. But she managed it.

And she stood in the valley. Here were the pharaohs' tombs, waiting for her. Susan hurried on, trying to ignore the gentle rustling and whooshing sounds she could hear.

It's just the wind, she assured herself as she hurried on.

Part of the valley was in deep shadow, and so Susan had to go a little slower to find the place she was looking for. She found a mound of torches when she tripped on one.

They've already started on Menkheperenre's tomb, she realized.

Susan grabbed as many as she could carry and lit a spark from the little flame, sheltered in its pot beside the pile.

Shielding the light of the torch, she hurried to the entrance to Akheperenre's tomb. The door was sealed, slammed shut and tied with an elaborate twist of rope, woven in a pattern and then sealed with wax. How would she ever duplicate this intricate pattern? Using her knife and bending close, she carefully slit the ropes on the back of the knot. *I'll stick them back together with wax and no one will ever know*, she hoped.

The crystal pull was on her now. She could feel it calling to her. "I'm coming. I'm coming," she whispered through her teeth as she worked on the knot.

Finally the knot came free, and in her eagerness, Susan dropped the rope to the ground and pushed on the door. To her relief, it opened without a sound, and holding her burning torch high above her head, she tiptoed into the tomb.

She placed the first torch in the sconce by the door and lit another. The air was still and dry, but

Susan heard skitterings, which turned her blood to ice. Turning, she reluctantly closed the door behind her so that her light wouldn't shine out into the valley.

"Crystal, come to me." Hopefully, Susan held out her hand. "Come, crystal, I am here," she said out loud. The echoes of her words grew around her and sounded loud in her ears. She could hear the sound traveling into the depths of the tomb, but no crystal came to her hand, although she still felt the pull.

I'm disturbing Pharaoh Akheperenre's rest, she thought, sadly. *I didn't want to do that.*

Susan began creeping along the gallery, holding her torch high. All was silence now except for her own quiet footfalls. The burning torch made the pictures on the passageway dance in the corners of her eyes. Susan shuddered to see, but she kept moving forward. Her crystal, her way home, was ahead of her. Everything else was secondary.

Susan ran one hand along the wall as she moved. A picture on the opposite wall caught her eye, and she moved across the gallery for a closer look. It was a picture of Akheperenre in his reed boat. He was hunting in the reeds. He was holding his boomerang-shaped throwing stick, and there were several birds draped over the side of the little boat. Another boat was drawn up beside the pharaoh's, and Susan could read that the first occupant of this boat was Djus. The second occupant of the boat was a girl, and peering closer Susan saw the inscription. "Merit-Amen, teller of mighty tales and a very good swimmer." Pharaoh Akheperenre had instructed that she be recorded in his tomb. This was a high honor and brought back memories of the happiest times Susan had had in Egypt with Akheperenre and Djus—and now she was stealing around in his sealed tomb.

Tears trickled from her eyes, and Susan sniffed in the quiet, feeling the loss of this great pharaoh all over again.

But her crystal pulled her on. She was torn in two. Stay in Egypt and lose her mother and father, who would never know what had happened to her, or, grab her crystal and go home and lose Djus and the wonderful life of Egypt. Either way she lost. Susan moved along the corridor.

Down a set of stairs and on. Darkness in front of her and behind, Susan traveled in the flickering cone of light thrown by her torch. Her hand on the wall felt a ridge in the stone. Susan stopped still, and her fingers crept along the ridge. What did it mean?

Susan crept forward slowly, puzzled by the ridge.

Thwang.

A spear shot out of the wall, pinning her cape to the floor. It took every ounce of courage Susan had, but she managed to freeze. She was stuck. Any movement could set off more spears. Now she remembered Harsheer's warning on her first visit.

Bit late, Susan, she berated herself. She stood crouched over. The position was uncomfortable, and the torch was a dragging weight on her arm.

Think, think, what set it off? Susan peered at the spear and tried to spot the place on the wall where it had been resting. Yes, she could see that—and now that she looked she could see others, their tips protruding from the wall just in front of her. Her crystal called her on.

To ease her arm, Susan carefully lowered her torch. There on the floor, thin ropes stretched from wall to wall, entering into grooves. If Susan hadn't slowed when she felt the ridge on the wall, the spear would be sticking out of more than her cloak right now.

Susan gulped a deep breath and forced herself to stay calm. Now that she could see the ropes that triggered the spears, she felt she could move forward again. As long as her feet didn't touch another rope trigger. She knelt and pulled the spear from the floor, freeing her cloak. Susan could stand straight again and sighed with relief. She took the time to drink deeply from her water skin. Peering ahead into the gloom, she felt she could place her feet carefully enough to prevent any more of the spears from releasing, but it was a risk.

She poked the spear in front of her, deliberately hitting the next rope trigger.

Thwang. The spear juddered into the floor in front of her.

Susan jabbed the next one, and reaching with the spear as far in front of herself as she could, she triggered the spears one by one.

The noise and the shooting spears took every scrap of Susan's attention as she picked her way through the thicket of spears. Not all shot out in a straight line, and she was glad to have the spear so that she could trigger them well in advance of her path.

The end of the spear tunnel was marked by another ridge in the wall, so Susan walked along more quickly but kept her hand running along the wall.

Another flight of stairs led her farther into the ground. Susan felt the weight of all the stone above her. The crystal called, and she hurried toward it.

Finally she reached the main chamber, and there, resting in the middle, was the sarcophagus of Akheperenre. Susan walked across the floor until she stood at his feet. Reaching out her hand, she felt the deep carving of the stone. It was cold to her hand, and she shivered. Being here in the presence of the mummy of Akheperenre in his palace on earth made her feel like an intruder.

"I'm sorry," she murmured. "I didn't want to break your peace. You were always good to me, and I'm sorry you died in such a horrible way."

She wiped at the tears on her cheeks. "I'll always remember you," she promised.

Susan eventually moved over to the niche where she could feel her crystal's call. Bending close and holding her torch tightly, Susan felt for the slight depression of the disguised niche.

Balling her fist she punched through and pulled away the cloth covering. Peering in, she saw her crystal. Crystals. There were six there. Six? Harsheer had told her they were growing four. Susan grasped hers—it felt so right in her hand, but the others all came, too. They were all joined together at the base. Each one was a different color, making Susan remember how the colors had danced in the liquid before they had set it here to grow. Susan grasped her crystal firmly in her fingers and snapped it off the base. It came easily, and she tucked it into the pocket of her cloak.

Next she tried the red and that came easily, too. The blue one, when she tried it, wouldn't budge. The green and purple ones snapped off easily and yet the yellow one remained stuck to the base with the blue one.

Susan pushed these two, the blue and the yellow, back into the niche. She had the four that she had expected. Mrs. Coleman had told her there were four.

Susan hurried back along the corridors and stairways, eager to escape the still, quiet tomb.

CHAPTER 49

CAUGHT

As Susan reached out her hand to push open the door of the tomb, she hesitated. *How long have I been here?* she wondered. *Have I been missed? What will happen now?*

She felt in her pocket for her crystal. The touch comforted her, and she pushed the door open, determined to face whatever came.

The bright sunlight dazzled her. She put her hand up to shade her eyes and leaned back against the door.

"There she is. I told you, vizier-to-be." Susan heard Harsheer. She groaned inwardly and pushed away from the door.

Djus was standing behind Harsheer, and he looked stunned. Harsheer hurried forward and grasped her arm. "Where are they? They're mine," he snarled in her ear and then spun her around. "Oh, woe, Mighty Egypt, that such sorrow should fall on your land."

All Susan could see was Djus's face. She had never seen such anger there. She shrank inside. Her heart felt like a shriveled pea. Her hand stole to her pocket. *I'll just go,* she thought. *Djus will be glad to see the back of me, and I'll be home.*

"Why, Princess Merit-Amen?" Djus's voice sounded choked. It came from deep in his throat, and the words sounded spat out. Susan looked at him more closely. There was hurt in his eyes.

I can't leave him like that, she realized. *He's my friend.*

Susan straightened her shoulders and shrugged off Harsheer's grip. She walked deliberately to where Djus stood and sank to her knees before him. She leaned forward and touched her forehead to the ground. Her youth lock swung forward over her shoulder and the faint tinkle of the little bells was the only sound she heard. Then a far-off hawk screamed over the cliff, and Susan could move again.

She sat back on her heels and looked up at Djus. "I owe you an explanation, Useramen." Her words sounded strangled in her throat. She harrumphed and tried again. "I want to explain, but my words are for you only, my friend," she said in a more steady voice.

Djus nodded curtly to her and spun on his heel and stalked into the shade of the overhanging cliff.

Susan rose shakily to her feet and moved to follow him, but Harsheer stood in front of her, barring her way. "He'll have you killed for sure, girl. Did you get the crystals? Give me the crystals, and I'll try to help you," he whispered urgently.

Djus was leaning against the cliff, watching them. Susan sidestepped Harsheer and walked slowly to join him against the cliff. What could she possibly say that would make him understand why she had disturbed Pharaoh's tomb?

"When Harsheer told me what you were doing, I wouldn't believe him," Djus said as she arrived beside him.

"What did Harsheer say I had done?" Susan asked, stalling for time.

"What you obviously did do," Djus retorted.

Susan sighed. She wanted to weep for their broken friendship.

"I loved Akheprerenre," she said softly. "He treated me like a daughter."

Djus jerked his head in a nod and moved to cross his arms. Susan noticed that his hands were shaking a little.

"The love of a parent for a child is a wonderful thing for both of them," Susan hurried on.

Djus nodded again.

"I have a mother and a father in a distant land," Susan pointed out.

Djus nodded again, and this time he met her eyes.

Holding his attention, Susan put every ounce of her conviction into her words. "The means for me to return to my parents was hidden in Pharaoh's tomb. I have to go home. My parents must be worried sick. They don't know where I've gone or what happened to me."

"I would help you go home. I would give you ships and soldiers. Your parents can come here," Djus said.

"Thank you, Djus. I know you would do that for me even now, but it isn't enough. You can't get from here to my parents with ships and soldiers." Susan held out her hand with the crystals in them. "You need these," she said.

Djus peered closely at her hand. He grunted. "What?" he asked.

He can't see them, Susan realized.

"Watch closely," she instructed, and as Djus peered closely at her hand, she began describing the crystals to him. "See the ruby one," she said, "and this is the amethyst. There are four of them here. Only one is mine, this one here that is clear."

Djus began nodding. "Yes, yes," he said in wonder, "I begin to see them. They are mighty."

Susan continued talking, softly explaining to Djus about how powerful the crystals were. "Ma'at wanted them created. Ma'at wants them used to help people and to keep the balance in the world."

Harsheer snatched at her hand, making a grab for the crystals. "She stole them from me," he yelled. "They're mine, and she stole them."

Susan managed to hold the crystals. She pushed her hands behind her back and pushed as far back against the cliff as she could.

Harsheer yelled, pleading with Djus to order her to give him the crystals.

The thought of Harsheer having the power of the crystals to use made Susan angry. She could see what harm he could do with so much power and his greedy ambition. All the words of the priestess of Ma'at came back to her. *He couldn't even see the crystals until I made them visible for Djus*, Susan decided.

"Wait," she stepped forward.

Djus and Harsheer turned to her. She took another step forward and carefully separated out her crystal from the other three.

She held them out. "If these are your crystals—as you say, and if you have the right to them—as you say, then take them if you can."

Susan threw the crystals out into the valley. They twinkled in the sunlight and then arced to the ground to fall among the shale on the valley floor.

Harsheer screamed and rushed out into the valley, scrambling on his hands and knees looking for the crystals. Susan could see one right by his knee and knew that they were safe from his greedy eyes. *Ma'at will provide guardians for them,* Susan knew.

A sigh turned her attention back to Djus. A smile played around his mouth, and the twinkle was back in his eyes. "Princess Merit-Amen"—he bowed ironically—"it is never dull in your company."

"Egypt is never dull," Susan retorted. She turned to take the path out of the valley, but Djus caught her arm.

"Harsheer made a big fuss about you opening the tomb before we came. The news will travel to the city before the midday meal is served."

"What can we do?"

"You have to go home. You have the means, and we will have to make it now."

With the moment at hand, Susan felt reluctant to go. Djus had been such a wonderful friend to her, and all the experiences of life over the last six months came flooding in on her.

"I'll tell everyone that I sealed you in the tomb as a punishment, so they won't question where you are."

Susan nodded slowly, and the two of them set off back toward the tomb entrance.

They slipped inside the door together.

Djus removed his honor necklet from around his neck. "Here, Susan, it always helps to have gold when you're balancing the world." He gently placed the string of gold beads around her neck. It fell heavily against the necklace of Ma'at that she always wore.

"Thank you, Useramen." Susan bowed. "That is a high honor. I will treasure it," she said.

Susan reached into her bag and drew out the little statuette.

"Harsheer used this to draw me to your time in the first place, so you can think of it as a little me that you can have as your friend always. Because wherever or whenever I am, Djus, I am your friend."

Susan pressed the little figure into Djus's hands. "I'll have it encrusted with gold," he said.

"It won't be so much like me then," Susan said.

The farewell was stretching the two of them as tight as a mooring cord, so Susan stepped back and pulled out her crystal.

She pictured her bedroom at home. She thought of how it had looked when she'd been pulled away from it. *Maybe the writing will be back on the paper now.*

"I want to go home," she said in English.

She felt the jarring smearing that she was used to. All sounds merged into one sustained note. Djus's face stretched and ran, and all the colors leeched away.

Susan looked to her hand where her crystal lay. It hopped from her hand and fell at Djus's feet. And she was spinning, spinning. "Stop, go back," she cried. But Susan span on. Her crystal was gone. Still spinning Susan clenched her fist – and felt a tickle in her palm. The note she could hear rose higher. She opened her hand and watched in wonder as her crystal gradually took shape in her palm until it was fully there, in her hand again. Thump. Susan landed on her bed.

She lay there, stunned. She was home. It was the twenty-first century. And everything was different. But she had her crystal again. *Of course,* she realized. *The Crystal of the North had to come forward in time to me. If I had just taken it from the tomb and brought it forward what would happen to all the good that Guardians had used it for in the thousands of years between then and now. It had to grow in my hand because it shrank when I was first traveling to Egypt.*

Toot. Toot. Her dad did that. The van was driving up to the house from the road.

CHAPTER 50

JASON

"Hi. Hi, everyone!" Susan heard Judy on the front porch. "Susan isn't up yet. I knocked and knocked on the door, but she didn't answer."

The van stopped. Susan leaped off the bed in a panic.

They're here. They're here.

She caught a glimpse of herself in the mirror as she rushed to the door. And stopped dead. An Egyptian princess stared back at her. Quick. Quick.

Susan slammed her carry bag under the bed. She grabbed her dressing gown from the back of the door and wrapped it around herself tightly. OK. She looked again. Oops, the collar of Ma'at was still around her neck. Off that came. OK. Now, she noticed the cobwebs sifted into her youth lock. Her youth lock! For so long it had been part of her that only now did she realize how extraordinary it looked to have most of her head shaved and just one long braid of hair. What could she do? It would have to go.

She heard car doors slamming.

Scissors. Scissors. Where were her scissors? Snip. She cut it off above the beads and bells. She held it in her hands for a moment. Sighed and tucked it into her top drawer for now.

Checking in the mirror again—she still didn't look right. She was still mostly bald. A hat. A hat. She pulled out one of her knitted winter hats and jammed it onto her head and down around her ears. Aaaah, her earrings. Out they came.

She checked the mirror again. Susan shook her head. That would have to do. She stepped for the door. Sandals. Sandals. She quickly kicked them off, and finally, down the stairs she ran.

Susan reached the foot of the stairs just as Judy thrust the door open and held it so that everyone could crowd into the entryway. Judy, then Susan's mum and dad, next Uncle John and Auntie Laura, and, coming in last, Jason.

All Susan wanted to do was grab her mum and dad and hang on tight. They looked just the same as when she left. So much had happened to her, while it was only the next morning for them. But there were all these other people.

Susan's dad smiled at her. "Looks as though you had a good sleep anyway," he said. "You remember Uncle John, don't you?"

Susan just stopped herself from bowing low. *Not here. Not here.* She looked around uncertain. He was so big and buff and smiled down at her with his arms wide stretched. Hug it was then. It felt warm and friendly. Uncle John planted a kiss on her cheek. And so then it was hugs all around. Aunt Laura next. And then Jason, standing there, looking at her, swinging a little backpack in his hands.

Jason was about her height, but pale and thin. He stood a little stooped over as though he were too tired to hold his own weight. Susan walked over to him and shyly gave him a hug, too. She could feel every rib in his back through his jacket. He sort of melted against her. She turned to lead him over so he could sit on the stairs, but she'd forgotten Judy.

"Why are you wearing a hat inside, Sue Sue?" Judy laughed. She leaned over and whisked off Susan's hat. Susan made a grab for it. Too late. Susan stood there in the middle of a circle of silently staring people. Embarrassed she put her hand up and rubbed it across her scalp. There was a slight skritching sound.

Jason was the first to move. He reached up. With his eyes fixed on Susan, he gently pulled off his cap. He was completely bald. "Chemo," he said. "It was kind of you to want to make me feel like I fitted in.

We can grow our new hair together." Now, Susan gave Jason another big hug, but gently, gently so as not to hurt him.

"We are going to be good friends," she said to Jason.

All the adults began moving again. They quickly started all the little tasks that helped people settle in. Susan and Jason sat on the stairs.

Judy quietly handed Susan back her hat. But Susan didn't put it on.

AUTHOR'S NOTE

Ancient Egypt has a culture that spanned over four thousand years and ended around two thousand years ago. What this means is that you could read a vast amount about Ancient Egypt, and it wouldn't agree with the time to which Susan traveled.

For example, there are no pyramids in this story. Susan never sees a pyramid, and yet for a large part of Egyptian history, they were a very important part of life.

Some of the names I have used have become the most common words in our time, but were actually introduced by later Greek pharaohs. In fact Pharaoh is a Greek term for the king but has become so common that I have used it here. Nile is also the Greek name for the great river which features so prominently in all Ancient Egyptian history.

Tuthmoses I is, they believe, the first pharaoh to be buried in the Valley of the Kings. So that the tomb Susan visits and the tomb of this story is only the second one to be dug in the valley.

Research and exploration is still ongoing in Egypt. They often find new tombs or decipher a newly found manuscript, which can offer new insights into a life. At the time of this writing, nobody knows for sure how Tuthmoses II died.

What I have tried to convey in Susan's adventures is a sense of what life would have been like in the time of Tuthmoses II and Hatshepsut.

If you are interested in learning more about this period in history, there are many, many books on offer.

BIOGRAPHY

G. ROSEMARY LUDLOW

G. Rosemary Ludlow grew up in Adelaide, Australia, where she taught school for many years. She loved teaching children to read. Her favorite thing to do was to tell them stories. History stories, geography stories, stories about spelling, or arithmetic—it all can be stories.

When she arrived in Canada, she worked in a truck factory and then a lumber company. Later she worked writing scripts for video productions. These led her into the airline industry, paper mills, and even an aluminum smelter.

Whatever Rosemary was doing, though, she always felt steeped in story. She realized that you can look at everything around you and it has a story.

She always wanted to share her stories with children, and now she is beginning to do so. The first book she published is called *A Rare Gift* and is the beginning of Susan's Crystal Journals. *Pharaoh's Tomb* is the second in the series.

Rosemary is busily plotting out book three now. It seems Susan is off to medieval Europe next. And who's that with her?

When Rosemary was asked to speak her favorite word, she said, "Imagine," and smiled.

G. Rosemary Ludlow is a storyteller.